"What is it?"

Isaac looked around as if checking to see if anyone was within listening range. Ellen saw that the others had left for the house porch and that he seemed relieved.

"I want to apologize," he said, surprising her.

"What for?" she asked. For the way he'd insinuated himself into her day?

"For how I treated you after I met Nancy."

She remained silent. She couldn't have been more shocked than if he'd announced that he would be marrying the next day.

Concern flashed in his gray eyes. "Will you forgive me?"

"I've already forgiven you, Isaac," she said. "Some time ago, in fact."

"Then we can be friends again?"

She gazed up at him, wishing that they could, while knowing that it wouldn't be wise for her to trust his friendship again. "I don't think that is a *gut* idea." She gave him a sad smile. "We can't go back to the way we were."

Isaac eyed her with sorrow. "We can't go forward and forget about the past?"

She shook her head. "I can forgive, Isaac, but I can't forget."

Rebecca Kertz was first introduced to the Amish when her husband took a job with an Amish construction crew. She enjoyed watching the Amish foreman's children at play and swapping recipes with his wife. Rebecca resides in Delaware with her husband and dog. She has a strong faith in God and feels blessed to have family nearby. Besides writing, she enjoys reading, doing crafts and visiting Lancaster County.

Loving Isaac

Rebecca Kertz

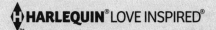
HARLEQUIN® LOVE INSPIRED®

Recycling programs for this product may not exist in your area.

 LOVE INSPIRED BOOKS

ISBN-13: 978-0-373-71983-9

Loving Isaac

www.Harlequin.com

Printed in U.S.A.

For by grace you have been saved through faith.
And this is not your own doing; it is the gift of God.
—*Ephesians* 2:8

For dear friends Pat and Mike Drexel, with love

Chapter One

The air was rich with the scent of roses and honey-suckle as Ellen Mast walked from the house to the barn. She entered the old wooden structure to get a bucket of chicken feed, then exited to release the birds into the yard.

"Here you go! Come and get it!" She smiled as she watched the hens and chicks scurrying toward the food. The lone rooster strutted out of the enclosure last, his chest puffing up when he saw the hens.

"Red," Ellen called to him as she tossed down a handful. "Over here. Come get it!" The rooster bent and ate, his red-crested head dipping toward the feed. "That's it. You always have to make an appearance last, *ja*?" She chuckled as she threw more grain, loving how the hens followed the trail wherever it landed.

"You'd better get down, Will, or you're gonna fall!" she heard her brother Elam exclaim.

"*Nay*, I won't!"

Ellen frowned as she skirted the barn toward the sound of her younger brothers' voices. She found them near the hog pen. Will was walking barefoot along the top wooden rail of the surrounding fence while Elam watched with dismay from several feet away. A number of pigs and hogs wallowed in the mud, while others snorted and stuck their noses into the wire fencing between the rails. She approached slowly. "Will!" she called softly so as not to frighten him. "You need to get off there."

Her brother flashed a guilty look. He teetered on the rail but managed to maintain his balance.

"Now," she said sharply when he made no effort to climb down.

Will shot her a worried glance. "El, I'm trying." He wobbled, lost his balance and fell into the mud pit. The hogs grunted and squealed as her brother scrambled to his feet.

Ellen dropped her bucket and ran. According to their father, their largest sow weighed close to five hundred pounds, while the rest weighed from twenty to two hundred. Fear pumped through her as she raced to unlatch the gate. "See if you can make your way, Will. Hurry!"

Will slogged through the mud, moving as fast as he could. The hogs and pigs grunted and squealed, the big one malevolently eyeing the intruder.

Ellen kept an eye on the animals as she held open the gate. After Will was out of danger, she shut and latched it, then scowled at him.

"You know better than to climb onto that fence or to do anything near the hogs except toss scraps to them." She stood with her hands on her hips, noting the mud covering him from head to toe. She wrinkled her nose at the stench. "*Mam's* not going to be happy. You stink." Fortunately, Will hadn't been wearing his hat and shoes or he'd have been in worse trouble with their mother.

"Ellen!" *Mam* called. Her mother waved her over to where she stood on the front porch of the farmhouse.

"Coming, *Mam*!" She hurried to put away her feed bucket, then quickly headed toward the house. Her younger brothers trailed behind—Will a sight covered in hog mud, with Elam walking some distance away, no doubt offended by the foul odor emanating from his brother.

As she drew closer, Ellen smiled at her mother. *"Ja, Mam?"*

"I need you to run an errand. The quilting bee is next week at Katie's. I'd like you to take our squares to her." *Mam* firmed her grip on the stack of colorful fabric squares as she leaned against the porch railing. "I promised to get them to her yesterday but couldn't get away—" Her mother stopped suddenly and looked past Ellen, her eyes widening. She inhaled sharply. "William Joseph Mast, what on earth have you been doing?"

"Walking the hog fence," Elam offered helpfully.

His mother frowned. "And you, Elam? What were you doing while Will was on the fence? Waiting for your turn?"

"Nay, Mam. I told him to get down but he wouldn't listen." Elam blinked up at her without worry. "And then he couldn't get down."

Her mother clicked her tongue with dismay as she turned back to Will. "Go to the outside pump and wait there, young man! You'll not be stepping into the house until you've washed and changed clothes." Her gaze didn't soften as she turned to her other son. "Elam, run upstairs and get clean garments for your *bruder*." Her lips firmed. "I'll get soap and towels."

"Mam?" Ellen asked softly. "Do you still want me to go to Katie's?"

"Ja." Her mother glanced at the fabric squares in patterns they'd stitched by hand and nodded. "Let me put them in a bag first."

Ellen left shortly afterward to the sound of Will's loud protests as *Mam* scrubbed the stinky mud from his hair and skin at the backyard water pump.

The day was clear and sunny, and the traffic on the main road was light as Ellen steered Blackie, the mare pulling her family's gray buggy, toward the Samuel Lapp farm.

Many of their women friends and neighbors would be attending the quilting bee at Katie Lapp's next week. Katie would stitch together the colorful squares that everyone had made at home. She would pin the length of stitched squares to a length of cotton with a layer of batting in between. Then she would stretch the unfinished quilt over a wooden rack from which the community women would work together, stitching carefully through all three of the layers.

Ellen enjoyed going to quilting bees. She had been taught as a young girl to make neat, even stitches and was praised often for them. After their last quilt gathering, *Mam* had confided to her on the way home that her work was much better than that of many of the seasoned quilters, who were often too busy nattering about people's doings in the community to pay much attention to their stitches. Her mother had told her once that after everyone left, Katie would tear out, then redo the worst of the stitches, especially if the quilt was meant to be given as a wedding present or sold at a community fund-raiser.

"Won't Alta know that Katie took out her stitches?" she'd asked her mother.

Mam had smiled. "*Nay*, Alta never remembers which area she quilted. She often takes credit for the beautiful work that Katie or you did, Ellen."

The memory of her *mam's* praise warmed her as Ellen drove along the paved road, enjoying the peace and beauty of the countryside.

The silence was broken when she heard the rev of an engine as a car came up too quickly from behind. A toot of a horn accompanied several young male shouts as the driver of the vehicle passed the buggy too closely without trying to slow down. Her horse balked and kicked up its pace and the buggy veered to the right. Ellen grabbed hard on the reins as the buggy swerved and bumped along the grass on the edge of the roadway.

"Easy, Blackie," she commanded, trying to steer the animal in another direction. She pulled hard on the leathers. The horse straightened, but not before the buggy's right wheels rolled into a dip along the edge of someone's property where the vehicle drew to a stop. The jerking motion caused Ellen to slide in her seat and hit the passenger door before smacking her head against the inside wall. She gasped as pain radiated from her forehead to her cheek. She raised a hand to touch the sore area as she sat, breathing hard, shaken by the accident.

"Hey, Amish girl!" a young male voice taunted. "Stop hogging the road!"

Ellen felt indignant but kept her mouth shut. She'd been driving with the awareness that if a car needed to pass her, it could. She'd stayed toward the right and left plenty of room.

She saw with mounting concern that the car had pulled over to the side of the road ahead and stopped. Four teenage English boys hung out the open windows, mocking her driving skills and the way she was dressed.

"Too afraid to wear something nice, huh?" one called.

"Why don't you let us see your pretty blond hair?"

They didn't ask, nor did they care, if she was all right. They apparently didn't worry that their actions might have caused her to be seriously hurt.

Her face throbbed and she was afraid to move. Her buggy was angled to the right, and if she shifted in the wrong way, then it might tip onto its side, causing damage to the vehicle and injuring her further.

The driver stepped out of his car. "Dunkard girl! Watch where you're going! Do I have to show you how to drive that thing?"

Ellen was suddenly afraid. What would she do if the boys came within reach of her? How could she protect herself if they surrounded her? Her heart pounded hard. She reached up to touch her face. Her forehead and cheek hurt. Her fingers burned from tugging hard on the leathers and her shoulder ached. She couldn't get out of the vehicle.

Her fear vanished and she became angry. She sent up a silent prayer for God to help her get over her anger quickly and to keep her safe from the English teenagers.

"What do you think you're doing?" a male voice called out to the *Englishers* from behind her.

That voice! Ellen recognized it immediately. He appeared next to her vehicle, confirming who it was. She frowned. Out of everyone within her church district, why did she have to be rescued by Isaac Lapp?

* * *

His heart thundered in his chest as Isaac watched the buggy bounce across uneven ground before coming to a halt in a ditch along the side of the road. The vehicle tilted at an angle and, alarmed, he raced toward the driver's side to see if he could help. He peered through the opening of the window. When he recognized Ellen Mast sitting on the far side of the front seat, he inhaled sharply. She held a hand to her forehead, and he spoke softly so as not to scare her. "Ellen? How bad are you hurt?"

She blinked pain-filled blue eyes at him. "I'm *oll recht*."

His lips firmed; he didn't believe her. He glanced ahead toward the car and stared at the driver as another boy climbed out the front passenger side. "Ellen, hold on tight while I pull your buggy back onto the road," he said gently as, ignoring them, he turned back.

"What are you doing here, Isaac?" a boy snarled.

Silently praying for control over his anger, Isaac faced the *Englishers* he'd once regarded as friends until he'd realized how mean the boys were. The group of friends was always asking for trouble. He moved toward the front of Ellen's horse and glared at the two boys. Brad Smith had caused enough pain and heartache to last him a lifetime. Isaac wasn't about to let the *Englisher* or any of his friends hurt anyone else in his Amish community, especially Ellen, a vulnerable young girl.

"Go home, Brad," he called out. "You've done enough damage for one day."

A third youth stepped out from the car's backseat. He stared at Isaac across the distance. "I wonder what

Nancy's going to say when she hears you've been hanging around that Aay-mish girl!"

Refusing to rise to their taunts, Isaac grabbed the mare's bridle and pulled the animal toward the road. The horse moved slowly with Isaac's steady pressure on the reins. Within seconds, he'd maneuvered the mare back onto the road. The buggy bucked and jerked as the right wheels rolled up the incline onto pavement. He felt Ellen's eyes on him as he calmed the animal with soft words, then returned to the driver's side of the girl's vehicle.

"Isaac!" the third boy snarled.

Isaac stiffened, then faced them. "Roy, go home—all of you! You could have caused her serious injury. If you don't want to get arrested, then you'd better go and leave us alone." Brad Smith and his friends were bullies who liked to pick on anyone who couldn't fight back. Fortunately, Brad didn't intimidate him. *I won't allow him to bully Ellen*.

"You know them?" Ellen murmured as the boys piled back into the car and left.

"Ja." He stared unhappily down the road in the direction they'd left before he turned, dismissing them.

"Who is he?" Ellen asked.

"Brad Smith. Nancy's *bruder*."

Nancy Smith. The name filled Ellen with dread. *The girl who ruined my friendship with Isaac.* Isaac had met the English girl during his *rumspringa* and liked her so much that he'd brought her home to meet his family. He'd taken her to a community gathering and a church service. If that wasn't disturbing enough, he'd brought her to a Sunday-evening community youth singing. Having the English girl in their midst had felt awkward for her. She and Isaac had been good friends until Nancy had learned of his friendship with Ellen and proceeded to monopolize his time. Isaac had been so enamored of her that he'd allowed it. He'd forgotten about Ellen. But Nancy hadn't. She had made it clear to Ellen that Isaac was hers and he no longer would have time for her. It had been a terrible loss for Ellen, as she had fallen in love with Isaac.

Thinking to do the right thing to protect her friend, Ellen had warned Isaac that the English girl was not a nice person. But, too blinded by his infatuation with Nancy, he'd refused to believe Ellen and had become angry with her. Ellen had felt betrayed by Isaac's reaction and his lack of trust. Ellen had loved him; she wouldn't have purposely set out to hurt him. If Nancy had been the good person she'd pretended to be, if she'd been kind and genuine, someone who could have made Isaac happy, Ellen would have kept her mouth shut. She'd thought she owed it to him to tell him the truth, but the truth had backfired on her. Not only did Isaac not believe her, he'd cut off all ties of their friendship.

I don't want to think about it, Ellen thought. The incident had happened over two years ago, and she mustn't dwell on it. As far as she knew, Nancy was no longer in Isaac's life. She had gone, but she left a friendship in tatters.

Ellen was fine and she'd moved on. Hadn't she been enjoying the company of Nathaniel Peachy, their deacon's son? Her friendship with Nate was an easy one. With him, she didn't have to constantly hide her feelings. They were friends and nothing more.

Besides, she had a new plan for her life. One for

which her parents hadn't given their approval, but it was something she'd begun to think of as God's calling for her. She wanted to work with special-needs Amish children, those born with genetic disorders. Her friends Rebekka and Caleb Yoder had a daughter who suffered from Crigler-Najjar syndrome, a genetic disease caused by a buildup of bilirubin—a toxic substance responsible for jaundice—in the little girl's blood. Fortunately, little Alice's condition was type 2. The child had to remain naked under a special blue LED light for ten to twelve hours a day. The treatment could be especially brutal on cold winter or hot summer days.

After visiting the Yoder home, witnessing the child's treatment, Ellen had felt something emotional shift inside her. Unlike little Alice, she'd been blessed with good health. She felt the powerful urge to help families like the Yoders with children like Alice.

The buggy suddenly jerked as it moved. Startled, she held on to the seat. She grimaced at the pain caused by the vehicle's sudden shift in movement. Soon the jerking stopped and Ellen sighed with relief as she felt the buggy wheels rolling on pavement.

She stuck her head out the window. Isaac had pulled her vehicle out of the ditch and back on the road. Fortunately, no other cars had been around to hinder the progress. As Isaac had said, the English boys were gone. She could no longer see them. She just had to get through the visit to Katie Lapp's and then she could go home.

Isaac climbed into the driver's side of her buggy. "Your wheels are out of the ditch." He stared at her, his brow furrowing. "Your head hurts," he said with concern.

"I'm fine." Ellen promptly dropped her hand and

lifted her chin. The movement made her grimace with pain and she turned to stare out the passenger window. She had to be grateful for his help, but she didn't want him here. "Why are you in my buggy?"

"I'm going to drive you wherever you're going."

"There's no need. I'm fine. I just need a minute."

He remained silent as he studied her. "Where are you headed?"

"To see your *mudder*." She gestured toward the bag that had fallen to the buggy floor during the accident. "*Mam* asked me to bring those—the squares we made for the quilt we're all making."

Isaac opened the door and met her gaze. "I need to check your buggy to see if it's safe to drive."

Ellen watched as he slid out of the vehicle. Despite the rising bump on her forehead, an aching cheek, a dull throbbing in her right shoulder and some red, burning fingers, she knew she was well enough to drive her vehicle. She kept silent as she waited for Isaac to finish checking the carriage for damage.

"Looks *gut*," he said to her through the passenger window opening within inches of where she sat. "I'd suggest that Eli take a look, but I don't see anything physically wrong with the structure. Still, you may want to think about taking it to him later to be sure."

"Oll recht."

He was too close. Ellen could see the long lengths of his dark eyelashes and feel the whisper of breath across her skin. He examined her with watchful gray eyes, and she shivered in reaction to the intensity of his regard. She moved to slide across the seat. His arm on her shoulder stopped her and she had to hold a cry so he wouldn't realize that she'd hurt it when she'd been thrown against the door.

"I have to go." Ellen shifted uncomfortably when he didn't move. To her shock, he reached out to lightly stroke her cheek.

"You're going to have a bruise," he said huskily as he withdrew his touch.

Ellen was powerless to look away from the intensity of his gray eyes, the tiny smile playing about his lips. "I *need* to go—"

"You're not driving."

She gazed at him, more than a little annoyed. "'Tis a buggy, not a car. I can handle it."

"Not in your condition."

She scowled. She didn't want to ride with him, with the man who hadn't trusted her. Why should she trust him to take her anywhere? She realized that she hadn't forgiven him for the past but at the moment she didn't care.

"Ellen?" Isaac frowned. "Tell me the truth. Your head hurts, *ja*?" His tone was gentle.

She closed her eyes at his kindness, wishing that she could turn back time to before things had soured between them. Did he honestly think that she'd forgotten what he'd done? Why was he acting like her friend again when it had been two years since he'd cut off their friendship?

"Ellen?"

"*Ja*, it hurts," she admitted rudely.

"You need ice for your cheek." His voice remained kind, making Ellen feel bad. "I was on my way home. Let me drive you." He leaned in through the open window and the scent of him filled her nostrils. Memories of an earlier time rose up and slammed into her. Her eyes filled with tears. She turned away so he wouldn't see them.

"Ellen…"

She blinked rapidly before she faced him again.

He reached out to touch her forehead, his finger skimming over the lump beneath the surface of her skin. His touch was light but she couldn't help a grimace of pain. His gray eyes darkened. "I'm driving," he said in a tone that brooked no argument.

Isaac left her to skirt the vehicle. He seemed suddenly larger-than-life as he slid in next to her. She didn't want him to drive her. She didn't want him anywhere near her. The way he was making her feel made her afraid, afraid that she wasn't over him, and despite the past and the way he'd chosen Nancy over her, she might still love him. It was better to stay angry with him. It was the only way to protect her heart.

With a click of his tongue and a flick of the leathers, Isaac urged the horse forward. Ellen sat silently in her seat beside him, and she could feel his brief side-glances toward her as he drove. She ignored them.

The remaining distance to the Samuel Lapp farm wasn't far. Ellen saw the Lapp farmhouse ahead as Isaac steered the horse onto the long dirt lane that ended in the barnyard near the house. He drew on the reins carefully, easing the carriage to a halt as if he worried about hurting her. He parked the buggy near the house, then jumped down from the bench and ran to assist before she had a chance to climb out on her own. She shifted too quickly in her seat and gasped with the searing pain. Her head hurt and her right shoulder, which had slammed against the buggy wall, was throbbing. She was furious at how weak she felt. She didn't want Isaac to be right. She didn't want Isaac to be the one she had to rely on, even if just for a little while.

Isaac appeared by her side and gently clasped her arm. "Easy, now, Ellen," he murmured. "Slowly."

She winced as she swung her legs toward the door opening. She made a move to step down until, with a sympathetic murmur, Isaac released her arm to encircle her waist with his hands. He lifted her as if she weighed no more than a young child. Ellen was conscious of his nearness, his male scent and the warmth of his touch at her midsection as he held her a brief moment before he set her down. Tears filled her eyes. Her injuries hurt but so did her aching heart.

"Danki." She didn't look at him as she stood there, feeling weak. Reaction set in. The horror of what those boys could have done to her caused her body to shake. She drew deep calming breaths, hoping he didn't notice.

"Ice. You need an ice pack," he announced as he bent to retrieve her bag from the buggy floor. He tucked it under his arm, then reached for her with the other. Fortunately, Ellen had regained control. "Come. Let's get you into the house." He slipped his right arm about her waist and helped her toward the house. Ellen wanted to pull away. She felt her heart thundering in her chest and grew worried that she'd lose control of her emotions again.

Chapter Two

"Ellen?" Isaac's mother had stepped out onto the front porch of the farmhouse. She frowned as she saw Isaac leading Ellen with his arm about her waist. "What happened?"

Ellen felt the sudden tension in Isaac's shoulders. "Some *Englishers* forced her off the road. The buggy came to a stop in a ditch."

"*Ach, nay.* Poor dear." Katie eyed her with concern. "Isaac, help her into the kitchen."

Ellen wanted to insist on walking on her own, but she wasn't about to protest in front of his mother. She still wasn't feeling the best and was grateful for the assistance. Her head hurt and she felt woozy.

"Here." Katie gestured toward a chair. "Sit her here."

Isaac saw her comfortably seated, then promptly disappeared into the back room.

His mother bent to closely examine her injuries. "You hurt your cheek." She narrowed her gaze as she studied her. "And your forehead."

Ellen nodded. Her cheek throbbed and she had a

headache. She reached up to feel the sore bump on her forehead.

Isaac returned and handed his mother an ice pack.

Katie smiled at him approvingly, then pressed it gently against Ellen's forehead. "Hold it here for a few minutes and then shift it to your cheek."

"Danki." She tried to smile until the simple movement of her lips hurt. Isaac stood by the kitchen worktable, watching silently.

"The driver was reckless," Katie said.

"Ja. 'Twas Brad Smith," Isaac said darkly.

His mother shot him a glance. "You know him?"

"Ja." Isaac's scowl revealed that he wasn't pleased. "He's Nancy's *bruder.*"

Katie frowned.

"Thank the Lord that Isaac came when he did," Ellen admitted. The memory of the boys getting out of their car made her shudder.

"I'm glad I was there to help," he murmured, his expression softening.

Ellen didn't say anything as she looked away.

"You did *gut, Soohn.*" Katie regarded her son warmly.

Something flickered in Isaac's expression. "Any one of us would have helped." He smiled. "You taught us well."

Katie nodded. "I'll put on the teakettle." She turned toward the stove. "You need a cup to revive you."

As she held ice to her cheek, Ellen encountered Isaac's gaze. She shifted the bag to her forehead. Isaac frowned, left the room and returned with another ice bag. She gave a jolt when he sat down close beside her and pressed it gently against her cheek. *"Danki,"* she murmured.

He leaned forward as he kept hold of the ice. "You're *willkomm*."

"Here we are." Katie set three cups of hot steaming tea on the table. She returned to get a coffee cake from the counter. "How about a nice slice of cinnamon cake? I made it fresh this morning."

Ellen had smelled it as soon as she'd entered the kitchen earlier. She felt her stomach rumble as if urging her to eat. Embarrassed, she nodded.

She lowered the ice pack and set it on the table. The ice was soothing to her injuries, but after a while, the cold felt too intense. Taking her cue, Isaac removed the other bag. She was aware that he watched her every moment as if he half expected her to faint or fall over...or something worse. She tried to smile reassuringly but the simple movement caused pain to radiate along the right side of her face. Without asking, Isaac quickly picked up an ice bag and held it to the painful area. Ellen welcomed the cold again, as it helped to alleviate the soreness. Disturbed by his nearness, she reached up to take control of the bag. Her fingers accidentally brushed against his; she froze as she locked gazes with him.

"I've got it," she assured him. She hated that he had the power to make her feel something besides anger, that he could still make her wish for things that she no longer wanted.

Isaac leaned back in his chair without a word as his mother sliced the coffee cake, then set the pieces within reach in the middle of the table. Katie then sat across from her and Isaac. In the ensuing silence, Ellen remained overly aware of Isaac beside her as she sipped from her teacup.

"Where's Hannah?" Isaac asked conversationally.

"At Abram's." Katie took a sip of tea. "She loves playing with Mae Anne."

Their deacon, Abram Peachy, a widower, had married Charlotte King of the Amos Kings, who lived across the road from the Lapps. When she'd married Abram, Charlotte had become mother to Abram's five children. Then a year and a half ago, Charlotte had given birth to a daughter, Mae Anne, and she had six children to mother and love. Mae Anne, a toddler, was as cute as she was bright, and her older siblings adored her. Isaac's sister, Hannah, now eight, had been drawn to the baby immediately. The youngest Lapp sibling loved spending time with babies and children younger than her, including her own nieces and nephews.

"She's *gut* with *kinner*. She'll make a fine *mudder* one day." Ellen dug her fork into the coffee cake and brought a piece to her mouth. She felt Isaac's gaze on her, met his glance and quickly looked away. She felt her heart rate accelerate, her stomach flutter as if filled with butterflies.

Isaac gazed at the girl seated at his family's kitchen table and felt his stomach tighten as he thought of the accident. When he'd learned that it was Brad and his friends in the car, he'd felt his hackles rise. These English boys were rude and nearly always up for trouble, and trouble was the last thing he needed. He'd already found it once with them, and he wasn't looking to get involved with them again. Except he'd never have known Nancy's true colors if not for them. He'd been happy when he'd met Nancy Smith, pleased when she'd wanted to meet his family. He'd found her fascinating, and after he'd spent some time with her, his fascination had grown. Dressed all in black, she'd worn heavy eye makeup and bright red lipstick. Her appearance stood out in a crowd, which wasn't the Amish way, but she'd been sweet and he'd realized after talking with her for hours that they shared a lot in common. Until he'd learned that she'd pretended to like him simply because she'd been curious about the Amish way of life.

The pain of learning the truth about her still lingered. His foolishness in getting involved with her and her unkind circle of friends bothered him. He'd given his parents cause to worry, and for that he was sincerely sorry.

As Ellen and his mother chatted, Isaac studied the young woman seated next to him. He had a clear up-close view of her features. Tendrils of blond hair had escaped from under her *kapp* during the accident. The bruise on her cheek stood out starkly against her smooth complexion. She turned, saw him staring and raised her eyebrows questioningly. He continued to watch her, unable to look away. Her cheeks turned bright pink and she averted her gaze.

It seemed impossible that they'd known each other forever, but they had. He had to admit it had been a long time since they'd spent any time together like they used to. His fault, he knew, but he couldn't undo the past. He'd chosen Nancy over Ellen.

Isaac experienced a strange tingle of awareness of Ellen that he'd never felt before. "How is your head?"

Ellen gingerly touched her forehead. "Not too painful."

He frowned, because he didn't believe her. He stood. "I'll get more ice."

"*Nay*, I'm fine." She waved at him to sit down.

He reluctantly resumed his seat. "When you're ready to go, I'll take you home."

"There's no need—"

"Let him, Ellen," *Mam* said. "You just had an accident. You shouldn't be driving home until you're certain there are no other aftereffects."

"I'll take you home," Isaac said. "Jacob can give me a ride back." It was an easy walk from Ellen's house to Zook's Blacksmithy, where his older brother Jacob worked.

"I don't want to be a bother."

"You're not, Ellen," he said, teasing her. "At least, not today." He paused. "Finish your cake. You need to keep up your strength."

She arched her eyebrows. "I don't need to eat. I'm strong enough."

"You don't like my *mam's* cake?" He laughed when he heard her inhale sharply, saw her expression fill with outrage.

She glared at him, but he could see that she fought a smile.

His mother had left the room. She returned within minutes with Ellen and her mother's quilt squares, which he'd placed on top of their hall linen chest on their way through to the kitchen. *Mam* pulled the squares out of the bag. "These are lovely, Ellen."

Ellen smiled. "I'll tell *Mam* that you said so."

"I see your work here. Your stitching is extraordinary."

Isaac was intrigued. "May I see?"

His mother chose and then handed him two squares. Isaac examined them carefully and thought he knew which one was Ellen's. "Your stitches are neat and even," he murmured and then held up the one in his right hand. "This one is yours."

Ellen seemed stunned. "How did you know?"

He shrugged. "I just did." And his mother had said that Ellen's work was extraordinary. He was unable to take his gaze off her, saw her blush. He returned the squares to his mother. "Who's getting the quilt?"

"Martha," *Mam* said. "For the baby."

Isaac smiled. His older brother Eli and his wife, Martha, were expecting their first child. "Doesn't Martha usually come to your quilting on Wednesdays?"

Mam smiled. "*Ja*, but she told me that she can't come this Wednesday. With hard work, we'll get her quilt done in one day."

He smiled knowingly. "You told Eli."

"I had to," *Mam* said defensively. "I couldn't risk that Martha would change her mind and decide to come." She rose to her feet. "I'll put these upstairs. Martha could stop by for a visit." She left with the squares and seconds later her footsteps could be heard on the stairs.

Ellen stared into her teacup.

He eyed her with concern. "You don't look well. You should see a doctor."

"Nay." She glanced up from her empty cup. "I'm fine."

He studied her with amusement. "You're too quiet."

"Quiet?" She appeared offended.

He laughed. "You *were* quiet."

She scowled, then winced as if in pain.

"Your cheek hurts." He clicked his tongue. "We have aspirin. I can get you some."

"Nay."

"Another cup of tea?" he asked.

"Nay." She shook her head and grimaced.

"You need to stop shaking your head. It hurts you." He stood. "Ellen—"

She blinked up at him. *"Ja?"* Her expression suddenly turned wary.

"You *will* let me drive you home," he said, his voice firm. He wouldn't take no for an answer.

Ellen relented. *"Oll recht,"* she said, surprising him. "After your *mudder* comes back."

He inclined his head. His *mam* returned and he waited while the women discussed refreshments for their Wednesday quilting bee. Finally, Ellen turned to him. "I'm ready to go now."

"I'll help you," he said quietly.

"I can manage on my own."

He frowned. He didn't like her coloring. She looked too pale. He exchanged meaningful glances with his mother. *"Mam*, we'll take the ice."

Mam nodded and handed the packs to Ellen.

Ellen accepted the ice bags graciously. They walked outside together until they reached the buggy.

"Ellen." Isaac extended his hand toward her. "I don't think we should take any chances." She took it reluctantly. He felt a jolt as he felt the warmth of her fingers. He helped her onto the vehicle's front passenger side. "Comfortable?" he asked huskily. He lingered, unable to withdraw his gaze.

"Despite my headache, sore cheek and throbbing shoulder?" she answered saucily. "I'm wonderful."

Her smart answer made him smile. "Shoulder?" He puckered his brow. "You hurt your shoulder and didn't tell me?"

"'Tis nothing."

He didn't believe her.

Her expression softened. "It doesn't hurt much."

Annoyed as well as concerned, Isaac rounded the vehicle, climbed in next to her, then grabbed the reins. As he drove silently down the dirt lane, then made a right onto the main road toward the Mast farm, Isaac found his thoughts fixed on the girl beside him.

Ellen stared out the side window as Isaac drove. *Why Isaac?* Why did he have to be the one who'd rescued her? She firmed her lips as she pressed the ice to her throbbing forehead. Her cheek hurt and she pressed the other bag of ice against her skin. She and Isaac had been such good friends. They'd walked often to Whittier's Store for a soda or an ice-cream cone. They'd talked about their families, their farm and their Amish community. She'd known that Isaac had looked at their relationship as just one of friendship, but Ellen had hoped that his feelings would change to become something more. She'd never told Isaac of her love for him. After what had happened with Nancy, she would have suffered the ultimate humiliation if she had.

After the accident today, she knew she could trust Isaac for help, as he'd helped her with the buggy and her injuries. But she could never trust him with her heart, not after the way he'd accused her of being mean-spirited and jealous of Nancy when she'd tried to warn him about the English girl.

Her fingers tightened on the bag of ice as she lowered it from her forehead to her lap.

She couldn't forget what she'd overheard that fateful day when Isaac, his brother and a few friends had been discussing Nancy—and her. She'd been coming around the side of the barn when she'd overheard them. She'd remained hidden, slowly dying inside as she listened to their conversation.

"Nancy is wonderful. I've never met a girl like her. I never thought I'd have a girlfriend like her."

"What about Ellen?" It had been Nate Peachy's voice.

"What about her?"

"I thought there was something special between you two."

Isaac had laughed. "*Nay*, it's not like that between us. She's like Hannah—my sister."

After hearing that, Ellen had run back the way she had come, her heart hammering within her chest, tears running down her cheeks. Thankfully, the boys hadn't seen her, hadn't witnessed the devastation she'd felt with Isaac's few simple words.

Isaac had abandoned their friendship and never looked back as he'd moved on with Nancy. Nancy had made it clear that Ellen wasn't needed in Isaac's life, and Isaac, by dismissing Ellen's fears, had agreed.

Ellen stared at the countryside as it rushed by her window. She couldn't help but remember the humiliation she'd felt the first time Isaac's friends had gazed at her with sympathy after his conversation about her with them. She hadn't wanted or needed anyone's pity. She still didn't want anyone's pity.

"You're quiet," Isaac said, interrupting her thoughts.

She met his gaze briefly. "I'm admiring the view." She paused. "I don't hear you saying much, either," she added with a lift of her eyebrows before she looked toward the window again.

He laughed. "True."

They had reached the end of the lane to her family

farm. She watched as Isaac expertly made the turn onto the dirt road. As he steered into the yard, he sent her a look, his eyes briefly focused on the side of her face. "Your cheek is turning purple."

"I'll live," she said flippantly. Regretful, she drew in a sharp breath, then released it. "I'm sorry. I guess it's hurting more than I'd like to admit. I appreciate what you did for me."

His eyes softened. "I'm glad I could help." He drove the buggy close to the barn and parked. Ellen climbed out of the vehicle before Isaac had the chance to assist her.

Her mother came out of the house. "Ah, *gut.* You're back. I need help with these pies for Sunday—" She stopped when she spied Isaac. "*Hallo*, Isaac. I didn't expect to see you."

"Josie," he greeted her with a nod. "I drove Ellen home because there was an accident with the buggy."

Her mother stiffened and studied her. "Are you hurt?" She turned to Isaac. "What happened?"

"A car passed too fast and spooked Blackie. The buggy swerved off the road," Isaac said. "Ellen did a *gut* job with controlling your mare. She kept the buggy from rolling over into the drainage ditch along Ned Yoder's farm."

Ellen felt self-conscious with the two of them studying her.

"You've hurt your cheek and your forehead." *Mam* looked with approval at the bag of ice in Ellen's hands. "You iced it—*gut.* Katie was wise to give it to you."

Ellen bit her lip. "It was Isaac's idea. He gave it to me." She didn't know why she told her mother that.

Her mother gave him a half smile. "That was kind of you, Isaac."

Isaac shrugged. "I was on my way home from Eli's when I saw it happen."

Ellen noticed that he hadn't told her about the English boys who'd forced her from the road.

"I should go." His gray gaze made an assessing sweep of her head and face. "You may want to keep that iced," he said softly.

She nodded. Although she had to fight the desire to tell him that she could do without his instructions.

"Will can take you home," her mother suggested.

"Will?" Ellen said with surprise. She frowned. "*Mam*, I don't think Will should be the one to drive him home."

"I'll walk to Jacob's as planned. I've been wanting to stop in and see him." He regarded her with a crooked smile. "Take care of yourself, Ellen." He turned to her mother. "Josie, I hope those pies you mentioned are for visiting Sunday."

Mam's lips curved. "They are."

Isaac grinned. "*Gut*. Something to look forward to." His gray eyes settled on her. "Be well, Ellen." He nodded to her mother. "Josie." Then he left, departing down the dirt lane toward the main road. She watched him for several seconds before she turned toward her mother, catching a glimpse of her parent following Isaac through narrowed eyes as he walked away. Ellen couldn't help but wonder what her mother was thinking. "Is something wrong?"

Mam shook her head. "I should get back to the kitchen."

"Pies?" Ellen reminded her.

Mam seemed to shake away her thoughts. "*Ja*. I've

promised to bring three pies this Sunday and I'm having trouble with them."

Ellen's lips twitched. Her mother was a good cook but for some strange reason pies weren't her strong point. Ellen's grandmother had been good at pie making and she'd taught Ellen.

Why did her mother choose to bring pies when they were clearly a chore for her? Ellen asked her.

"Alta Hershberger asked me to," she said simply, and Ellen understood. Her mother wouldn't challenge a request from the village busybody. To do so would give Alta fodder to natter about.

As she followed her mother into the kitchen, she immediately saw the mess *Mam* had made. She grinned. "How many piecrusts did you attempt to make?"

Mam looked sheepish. "One."

"Then we'd better get busy if we're going to bake three pies."

As she mixed the ingredients, then rolled out the crust dough, Ellen thought of her morning and Isaac's part in it. She frowned as she carefully lifted a rolled circle of dough and set it into a pie plate. The fact that Isaac had helped her didn't mean anything. It didn't mean he wanted them to be friends again.

Maybe it was time to go out and have some fun. She'd talk with her parents about going on *rumspringa*. Then while out and about, she could locate Dr. Westmore's medical clinic for genetic diseases. She needed to learn as much as she could to convince her parents to allow her to volunteer her time there.

Chapter Three

Sunday arrived, and Ellen climbed into the family buggy with her parents and younger brothers. The pies she'd made with her mother had come out nicely. The scent of baked apples, cherry and custard filled the vehicle, making her stomach grumble. Ellen was particularly pleased with the *snitz* and custard pies. Those were her favorite flavors, and she looked forward to enjoying a tiny sliver of each after the midday meal.

They were headed to Cousin Sarah's house. Sarah was married to Jedidiah Lapp, Isaac's oldest brother. Ellen knew that she'd probably see Isaac there, but she wasn't going to let it concern her. She'd had a couple of days to put things in perspective. She realized that it had felt odd to spend time alone with him again, the first time since before he and Nancy had begun seeing each other. *He's acted as if we've never had words over his English girlfriend.*

Now that she was on the mend, things would get back to the way they'd been before her buggy mishap. Isaac wouldn't notice her, and he'd leave her alone. Ellen looked forward to her first outing during her *rum-*

springa, the running-around time during which teenagers within the Amish community were allowed the freedom to enjoy the English world. It was their parents' and the community's hope that given the choice, their young people would make the decision to join the church and stay in the community. If they chose to leave, they were free to go and return to visit as long as they hadn't joined the church first. If they joined the church and then left for the English world, they'd be shunned by their families and friends and wouldn't be allowed to return.

Ellen had every intention of joining the church, but she wanted to enjoy *rumspringa*. She'd use the opportunity to check out the Westmore Clinic for Special Children, bring home information so that she could convince her father to allow her to volunteer there. She decided that she'd talk with her friend Elizabeth to plan a trip into the city of Lancaster. They could go next Saturday. The thought of getting away for the day excited her. She hadn't spoken to her parents about it yet, but she couldn't see why it would be a problem.

They arrived at the Jedidiah Lapp farm, where *Dat* steered Blackie onto the driveway and parked in the yard on one end of a long line of familiar gray buggies.

Sarah came out of the house, carrying her son, Gideon, as Ellen climbed out of the buggy with two pies.

"Sarah!" She always enjoyed spending time with her cousin. She and Sarah had shared a room when Sarah had first come for a visit, and Ellen had loved having her stay. She'd been pleased when Sarah, originally from Kent County, Delaware, had moved permanently to their village of Happiness after she'd fallen in love and married Jedidiah Lapp.

"Ellen." Sarah beamed at her, then greeted her aunt, Ellen's mother. "Josie, 'tis *gut* to see you. We haven't had time to spend together lately."

Her mother held a pie and made to grab one from Ellen, who smiled as she shook her head. "You're looking well, Sarah," *Mam* said. "Your little one is certainly getting to be a big boy."

"*Ja*, he is. I don't know where the time has gone. It seems like only yesterday that he was a newborn and now he's three years old."

Holding two pies, Ellen asked her cousin where she wanted her to put them.

"Jedidiah is getting a table. Would you like to set them inside until the table's ready?"

"*Nay*, I'm fine," Ellen said, studying Sarah's little son, who gazed at her with a big sloppy grin. "I'll wait."

As soon as Sarah set her son down, Gideon immediately ran to Ellen for attention. Her cousin quickly grabbed Ellen's pies so that Ellen could reach for him. "Want to go for a little walk, Gid?"

"*Mam*, can I?" Gideon asked his mother in Pennsylvania Deitsch.

"*Ja*, you may walk with Cousin Ellen, but you must be a *gut* boy."

The child nodded to his mother, then to Ellen who scooped him up for a hug.

"Be careful, Ellen," Sarah warned. "My *soohn* is no lightweight."

"*Ja*, he isn't." Ellen smiled at the dark-haired child as she set him on his feet. "We'll walk side by side—*ja*, Gideon?" She extended her hand and the child grabbed it and held firm as they headed toward the back farm field.

"Where shall we go?" she asked him.

"Goats," he said.

"You want to see the goats?" When he nodded, she grinned at him. "Let's visit your goats, then."

Isaac left the house with Jedidiah, carrying the table Sarah wanted outside. He looked across the yard as they negotiated the last of the porch steps to discover his sister-in-law Sarah with Josie Mast. He glanced about but didn't see Ellen anywhere. He was strangely disappointed. He was wondering how she'd fared since the accident, whether or not the bump on her forehead had changed color like the bruise on her cheek. Then he heard a giggle and spied Gideon running from Ellen, who chuckled as she ran across the yard after him.

"Come back here, Gideon!" she called laughingly.

"Set it down a minute, Isaac," Jed said. "I need to speak with Sarah."

Isaac silently set down the table. He watched as Jed approached his wife to say a few words with her. He saw Sarah gesture toward the back lawn.

It was visiting Sunday. Community folks were milling about the yard and inside the house, family and friends of Jed and Sarah. He heard voices from near the barn, where two men whom he recognized as church elders were joined by a newcomer he didn't recognize.

The sound of a squeal made him smile and turn back to watch Ellen and his nephew as Gideon ran from Ellen, the child's shriek of laughter evidence of his enjoyment of her chase. By her expression, he could tell that Ellen was having as much fun as Gideon. She laughed as she caught up to him and snatched him into her arms. When she began to tickle the boy's ribs, Gideon burst out into childish giggles. Isaac stared, fascinated by their play, and found his lips curving in response.

Jedidiah returned and picked up the end of the table. "My son is enjoying himself. Ellen will make a *gut mudder* one day."

A *mudder*? She was too young to be a mother. Without saying a word, Isaac shot her one last quick glance. His gaze locked with Ellen's briefly as she set Gideon down, then turned away. He focused his attention on moving the table.

"Sarah wants it there," Jed said with a nod of his head.

"Close to the house, near the back door?" Isaac guessed.

"*Ja*, she says it'll be easier for the women to bring out the food."

They carried the table to the designated area. After the brothers had set the table in place, their parents arrived. Isaac followed Jedidiah to greet them. He reached for the platter of cupcakes and cookies in his mother's arms.

"Where's my *grosssoohn*?" *Mam* asked when Isaac had returned after putting the dish on the table.

"He's playing with Ellen." Jedidiah grinned as his son ran away from the young woman, who laughed as she took off after him.

Gideon saw his grandmother and raced toward her. Unaware, Ellen gave chase, looking eager to catch the little boy.

"G'mammi!" the child exclaimed as he threw himself against *Mam*.

Ellen saw Katie and halted a few feet away. "Now

I know why he was running this way," she said with a grin.

"He's having a *gut* time with you, I see," *Dat* said.

"I've been having a *gut* time myself, Samuel."

"You like children," Isaac commented, unable to help himself.

She stiffened as if she'd just realized that he was there, but then he saw her relax as if she'd come to accept his presence. "*Ja*, I do."

They chatted for several minutes about Katie and Samuel's grandchildren and how much all of them had grown. Then Jedidiah picked up his son and accompanied their parents toward the house, leaving Isaac alone with Ellen.

He studied Ellen intently. "Your bruises... Your cheek looks better, but now you have one on your forehead." He paused. "You're feeling better?" he asked softly.

She nodded. "*Ja*, much better."

He looked at her approvingly. *"Gut."*

Sarah approached. "Ellen, may I talk with you for a moment?" She waved Ellen to follow and the two women moved away to chat privately.

Isaac wondered what they were discussing. He saw Ellen nod with a smile and Sarah grin, looking pleased.

"I think Sarah is asking Ellen if she'll help out after the baby comes," Jedidiah said softly as he rejoined Isaac.

Isaac glanced at his brother with surprise. "You mean Sarah's...?"

Jed beamed. *"Ja."*

"God has blessed you, *Bruder*." Isaac was pleased

for his oldest brother, who dearly loved his wife and son. "I'm happy for you."

His brother looked at him. "One day you'll have a family of your own."

Isaac shook his head. "Not anytime soon. I learned a hard lesson with Nancy."

"The *Englisher* was never like the girls in our community." Jedidiah hesitated. "We were worried from the start that she'd hurt you."

Isaac felt his stomach tighten. "I never knew you felt that way. You were all kind to her."

"And why wouldn't we be? You liked her. We hoped we were wrong, but she didn't seem as involved in your relationship as you."

Isaac sighed. If only he'd been smart enough then to realize the truth—that Nancy never cared for him. He thought of Ellen and recalled the friendship they'd once shared. Fool that he was, he'd tossed it away in favor of Nancy, believed Nancy over her when Ellen had wanted only to make him see Nancy's true nature.

Too many regrets. He didn't want to talk or even think about Nancy any more. She was gone, and he was glad. Jedidiah was an astute man and he let lie the topic of his past relationship with her.

Sarah and Ellen approached. "We're going to see to lunch. Either one of you hungry?"

"I am," Jed said.

Sarah gazed at him with affection. "You're always hungry."

"Always for your cherry pie."

"I didn't make a cherry pie for today."

"I made a cherry pie," Ellen said with a smile.

Jed's dark eyes lit up, and Isaac groaned as he shook

his head. "What is it with my *bruders* and their sweets?" he groused.

Ellen raised one eyebrow. "You don't care for sweets?"

"I like them well enough, but my older *bruders* are obsessed."

"You don't like *snitz* or custard pie, I imagine," Ellen said.

"Custard pie?" Isaac asked. He enjoyed custard pie.

"Vanilla custard." She looked amused.

"I like custard pie. You made one?"

She nodded. "Too bad you don't like sweets. Fortunately, there are plenty of folk here who will be happy to eat my custard pie." She walked away with a laugh and Isaac could only stare at her. A small smile curved his lips and he chuckled. *I deserved that. But if she thinks I'll not be getting a slice of that custard pie, she is mistaken. She's yet to learn how determined I can be to get what I want.*

It wasn't long until food was put on the table that he and Jed had set in the backyard. Besides the Masts and his own family, the Kings, the Peachys, the Zooks, and Alta Hershberger and her two daughters had come to share their visiting day. This was Jed and Sarah's first gathering at the farm. Watching his sister-in-law move among her guests, Isaac felt admiration for Sarah's ease with having so many people at her home. He wondered if he'd ever have a place where he could invite family and friends and feel so comfortable with them. Ever since the night when Whittier's Store was vandalized by Nancy's brother and his friends, he hadn't known a moment's peace. He'd taken the blame for something he didn't do, not because Nancy had asked him to—although she had—but because he'd been protecting a male friend, another member of their Amish community. Other church members, he knew, now looked at him with disappointment. It bothered him that they'd never questioned whether or not he could have been guilty, but just accepted that he was. He didn't feel less in the eyes of his family. His mother and father were supportive of all of their children, but he couldn't help feeling as if he'd let them down, too.

He'd hoped that his friend Henry would come forward and confess his part in the Whittier's Store debacle. But Henry had kept silent and remained noticeably absent from the community and Isaac's life. Apparently afraid to speak up after seeing how the community reacted to Isaac's guilt, Henry must have been unable to bear what would happen if he were to admit that he was one of the guilty parties.

No one is more disappointed with me than I am, Isaac thought. By taking the blame, he had effectively lied. And that was what made it difficult for him to stay in Happiness. As hard as it would be to live out in the English world, it might be better than living here without joining the Amish church. And how could he join the church when he didn't feel worthy?

Seeing Ellen with his nephew made him think of simpler, happier times when he and she roamed the countryside together as friends. He'd made a terrible mistake when he'd taken up with Nancy, Brad and their English friends. Now he was destined to pay for it.

Ellen did what she could to help Sarah put out lunch before she went in search of her friend Elizabeth. She was eager to go *rumspringa* and she wanted Elizabeth to go with her. She found Elizabeth with a group of young people, including the Peachy siblings and Peter Zook, who had congregated near the pasture fence.

"Elizabeth," she called as she approached. Her friend's eyes brightened when she saw her. "May we talk?" Ellen asked.

Elizabeth said something to the group before she joined Ellen, who stood on the outskirts several yards away. "Is there something wrong?" her friend asked.

"*Nay*, I want to go into Lancaster next Saturday."

Her eyes gleamed. "A *rumspringa* adventure?" Elizabeth asked.

"*Ja*. Would you like to go?"

"*Ja*." Elizabeth nodded vigorously. "What should we tell our *eldre*?"

"The truth," Ellen said, hoping her parents would approve.

Her friend agreed. "What will we do?"

"Shop? Eat? See a movie?" Ellen grinned. "Whatever we want to do." *Check out the Westmore Clinic for Special Children*, she thought.

After talking with her friend, Ellen grew more excited about the trip and couldn't wait to ask her *mam* and *dat* for permission. But she decided to wait until later to approach them.

"*Dat, Mam*," Ellen said after they had returned from Jedidiah and Sarah's house and everyone had settled in at home. "I'd like to go into Lancaster with Elizabeth next Saturday."

Her father frowned as he faced her. "Why?"

Ellen felt her belly flutter with nerves. "We want to go on *rumspringa*. I'm old enough to experience the

English world. We thought we'd get something to eat and wander about the outlet mall."

"I don't know if that's a *gut* idea—" *Dat* began.

"I don't see why you can't go," her mother said at the same time that her father spoke. *Mam* immediately grew silent. She wouldn't go against her father's wishes.

Ellen's spirits plummeted. Her *dat* wasn't going to allow her to go.

"She is old enough, William," *Mam* said gently, much to Ellen's shock.

Dat narrowed his gaze as he studied his daughter. "*Nay*, she can't be."

"I'm seventeen, *Dat*."

Her father looked surprised. "You are?" He firmed his lips. "You've grown up too fast."

Ellen noted his surprise with amusement. "You still have plenty of time with the boys. They are a long way from *rumspringa* age."

"Why now, *Dochter*?" he asked seriously. "Do you plan to leave our community? Are you unhappy here?"

"*Nay, Dat*. I have no plans to leave, but I want to see the English world. Just because I want to see it doesn't mean I don't want a life here…a husband and family."

"How will you get there?" *Dat* asked, looking relieved.

"May I take the pony cart? Or we can hire a driver to take us."

Her mother leaned close to whisper something in *Dat*'s ear. Her father nodded and said, "You may go next Saturday, Ellen, but I will hire a driver for you."

Ellen beamed at him. *"Danki, Dat."*

"Just come home safe and sound with no ideas of wanting to leave us," he warned. Ellen shifted uncomfortably as she thought of the clinic and her reason for visiting. Would her father and mother be upset after her return when she presented them with more information in an attempt to convince them to allow her to work there?

That night as she lay in bed, Ellen thought of the fun she'd enjoyed with her cousin Gideon and then her excitement as she and Elizabeth had discussed their Lancaster trip. She tried not to think of Isaac, with whom she'd spoken only briefly. It had been nice of him to inquire about her injuries. She'd been disturbingly aware of how he'd continually watched her.

Next Saturday, she thought with a smile, dismissing Isaac from her mind. She couldn't wait for Saturday's adventure with Elizabeth.

Chapter Four

Monday and Tuesday went by quickly as Ellen did her regular chores, including washing clothes and hanging the laundry on the line to dry. Wednesday morning she and *Mam* headed to Katie's house for their monthly quilting bee. It was a glorious day. The sun was bright in a clear azure sky and the spring blossoms looked pretty in the Amish and English yards they passed. Ellen wondered if she'd see Isaac today and decided that she wouldn't let the prospect bother her. Odds were that he would be out working with Samuel in the fields or with Jedidiah for Matt Rhoades, who had recently started his own construction company. In any event, even if she did see Isaac this morning, it wouldn't be for long. There was no reason for her to feel anxious or nervous. He had helped her last week, she had thanked him politely and she was fine. It wasn't as if she were in danger of falling for him again. The only reason they'd spent time in each other's company was that the circumstances of her accident had forced it upon them.

"How many do you think will come today?" she asked her mother.

"About ten, I suppose, as usual, with the exception of Martha."

Ellen smiled as she thought of the baby quilt they would be working on today. It wasn't large enough for a double bed. With the ten women working on it, the quilt would be completed in no time.

"*Mam*, don't you think it's going to be a bit crowded around the quilt rack if ten women show up?"

Her mother frowned as she maneuvered the buggy into a turn. "Hadn't given it any thought."

"If there are too many, I can do something else."

"*Nay*. Katie would rather have you stay than some of the others."

Driving past, Ellen waved to Annie Zook as she exited Whittier's Store. The young woman's face lit up as she acknowledged Ellen's wave with her own. She had EJ, her son, and her baby daughter, Susanna, with her.

"Are you coming to quilting?" Ellen called as *Mam* slowed the buggy and steered toward the right to allow a number of cars to pass by safely.

"*Ja*, I'll be there after I get these little ones home," Annie answered. "*Mam* said she'd stay back to watch them today."

"Why not bring them?" Ellen suggested. "Won't Hannah be there?"

"*Ja*, and Daniel," Annie said, referring to her brother-in-law. "I'll talk with *Mam*."

Once the roadway was clear, her mother drove back onto the road and continued on.

Ellen smiled as she glanced back to see Annie put her children into the buggy. "She looks happy," she murmured.

Mam flashed a smile. "*Ja*, she is. Jacob has been *gut*

for her, and I'm glad she finally understood that. He's loved her since he was a young boy."

Ellen raised her eyebrows. "He has?"

"*Ja*, and he nearly gave up. Annie fell for Jedidiah and Jacob thought that he didn't have a chance with her. Later, after Jed found Sarah, Jake hoped for another chance."

"How do you know all this?"

"Katie and Miriam, although Miriam wasn't keen on it at first."

Ellen reached up to straighten her *kapp*. "Why not?"

"That was right after Horseshoe Joe had his accident. She wanted someone who was financially able to take care of Annie. Someone like Ike King."

Ellen shuddered. "He was too old for her." She thought of Martha. "He was too old for Martha, too, but she married him anyway. She genuinely cared for him, didn't she?" She studied her mother to gauge her reaction.

"I believe she did." *Mam's* lips firmed. "'Tis too bad he passed on, but it must have been God's plan. I've never seen her as happy with Ike as she is now with Eli."

Ellen had to agree. She'd never seen such joy in Martha's brown eyes during the year she'd been married to Ike. Still, she was sorry that Ike had passed on. He'd been a nice man and Amos King's younger brother. And he'd been wonderful to Martha. They had all taken comfort that Ike was in the Lord's hands and thus resided with Him in heaven.

There were two buggies in Katie's barnyard as *Mam* pulled in and parked. No one was in the yard as they climbed out and retrieved the food dishes they'd made to share with the other women. She had made lima beans in tomato sauce and lemon chiffon cake. *Mam* had made chocolate brownies and macaroni salad. There would be plenty to eat today, more than enough to share with any of the male Lapp family members who might come in for lunch.

For a moment, Ellen's thoughts dwelled on Isaac Lapp. She wasn't alarmed that she'd thought of him; after all, this was his home.

Katie's door opened immediately after *Mam* knocked. Ellen felt her heart skip a bit as she caught a quick glance at the man who stood there. *Isaac.* The image of Isaac flittered away and she realized that it wasn't Isaac waiting patiently for them to enter. It was Joseph, the youngest brother. He was the spitting image of his older brother until she looked closer and saw the difference in eye color and the shape of his mouth. Joseph had younger, less mature features. Still, he was a handsome boy and would one day become an extremely attractive man.

"*Hallo*, Joseph," she greeted after *Mam* had gone in first.

"Ellen." He nodded. "My *mudder* and the others are in the gathering room." He glanced down at the food in her arms and finally smiled. "You've brought lemon cake."

"*Ja.*" She stepped past him and waited while he closed the door. "You like lemon chiffon cake."

"*Ja.*" His smile became a grin. "Looking forward to midday meal today." He stared at her cake plate. "I can take that for you."

"*Oll recht.*" She handed him the cake plate and Joseph disappeared into the back kitchen area. She heard someone coming down the steps from upstairs and looked up, expecting to see Katie or Hannah, her daughter. She froze. It was Isaac.

"*Hallo*, Ellen," he greeted as he approached. He narrowed his eyes as he studied her face. "Your forehead's turned a light shade of purple. Is it sore?"

"I'm fine."

"That's not what I asked you."

She sighed. "A little."

"How is your cheek? Can you smile yet without grimacing?" he teased. "Or does it still hurt?"

"What are you doing here, Isaac?" she said stiffly. She wasn't in the mood for his teasing or his questions about her health. "I thought you'd be working."

"Disappointed?"

She stared at him, wishing he would leave.

"I'm going to work soon. We've been waiting for the plumber to finish. Matt's picking Daniel and me up on his way to the job site." He glanced toward the staircase. "Daniel! Matt's going to be here any minute."

"Don't let me keep you," Ellen said tartly, and Isaac looked at her with an odd little smile.

"Ellen?" *Mam* called as she reappeared, peeking her head from a doorway. "We're ready to start. You'll want to get a good seat."

"Coming!" She turned back to Isaac. "Have a *gut* day at work, Isaac," she said, trying to be more polite.

Joseph returned from the kitchen. "I hid the cake in the back room," he confided with a grin.

"*Gut* thinking, Joseph," Ellen said with a chuckle. Isaac arched an eyebrow in question. "Lemon chiffon cake," she explained. "Apparently, it's your *bruder*'s favorite. He's protecting his fair share."

Eager to escape, she left him to join her mother in the gathering room, where Katie Lapp and several other women were seated around the quilting rack. She didn't know how long it would be before Matt Rhoades picked up Isaac and Daniel. Ellen tried not to think about Isaac at all as she greeted the other ladies in the room.

"Over here, Ellen." Katie gestured toward a seat between her and *Mam*. "I'm glad you've come."

"I enjoy quilting."

Mae King, who lived across the road, sat directly in front of her. On either side of Mae were her married daughters, Charlotte Peachy, who'd married their deacon, and Nancy Zook, who'd married Annie's brother Josiah. Ellen was pleased to see these young women, who were always pleasant and fun. She was disappointed that Elizabeth and her mother weren't here. She'd hoped to have a few private words with her friend about their outing on Saturday. She didn't know if Elizabeth's parents had agreed to let her friend go.

The six of them chatted for a while, and Katie offered them iced or hot tea. Ellen chose the iced tea, as the gleaming iced tea pitcher sitting on the table looked inviting as well as refreshing, and since it was a glorious day and the windows were open, it seemed the best choice.

"We saw Annie on our way over," she told Katie. "Coming out of Whittier's. Said she was going home to drop off EJ and Susanna and then she'd be here."

"Miriam offered to watch them," Katie said. "I wish they'd all come. Hannah is here to care for them—and Joseph."

Ellen felt her face turn red. "I'm glad you said that. I'm afraid I may have overstepped when I suggested the same thing." She felt relieved as she saw pleasure come to Katie's expression. "I thought that Daniel would be here. I didn't think of Joseph."

"He's certainly a grown-up young man," *Mam* commented. "How old is he now?"

"Eleven."

Ellen shook her head in wonder. Would he continue to look exactly like Isaac when he got older?

Elizabeth and her mother arrived to join the quilting bee gathering, and moments later Miriam Zook came with Annie and her two children.

"You've brought them," Katie gushed. *"Gut."*

"I didn't think about Hannah and Daniel," Annie admitted. "And I wanted to spend the day with my *mudder*, too."

Miriam glanced fondly at her daughter. "Are Hannah and Daniel here?"

"Hannah is," Katie said. "And Joseph. I don't think he'll mind watching EJ." She got up and left the room, then returned with her daughter and son.

"EJ!" Joseph exclaimed, his eyes lighting up with pleasure. "Would you like to go out and play?" He shot a look to his sister-in-law, who nodded. "Come on, buddy. Let's go see the animals in the barn."

Hannah was more than happy to stay with Susanna. She spread a quilt on the floor not far from the women and sat, setting the baby next to her.

Conversation started to buzz as the women threaded their needles and got to work.

"Alta's not here?" Elizabeth's mother asked.

"She's not coming today," Miriam said. Alta Hershberger, the resident busybody, was her sister-in-law, although Alta's husband, Miriam's younger brother John, had passed on when their two daughters were nine and ten. "She said she needed to go to market with Mary."

Annie glanced at her mother with raised eyebrows but didn't comment.

The women stitched for a couple hours before Katie stood. "Let's eat."

Mae King and Miriam got up to help their hostess with the food. Ellen started to rise to join them, but Katie waved her to her seat. "Sit. We'll manage."

The work on the quilt was progressing nicely. The stitches were neat and even. Ellen knew the women hoped to get most of it done today.

Elizabeth's mother rose with *Mam* and the two went into the kitchen to help the others. Ellen slid over to the seat next to Elizabeth.

"Are you allowed to go on Saturday?"

Elizabeth frowned. "*Nay. Dat* said I wasn't ready." She sighed dramatically. "What does he mean by that? I'm old enough."

Ellen stifled her disappointment. She didn't want to make her friend feel worse. "Maybe we can try again in a couple of months." She really wanted to visit the clinic, not that she'd said anything about it to her friend.

Ellen changed the subject and the girls chatted briefly about their siblings. Soon the women had the food ready, and following Elizabeth, she went to grab a plate. After eating lunch, the women went back to work and finished up at three thirty. There'd been no sign of Isaac or Daniel, who apparently had both gone to work with their older brother Jedidiah and Matt Rhoades.

Ellen felt immense relief when she and her mother headed home. She'd spent a large part of the day at the Samuel Lapp farm and had made it without encountering Isaac more than once. She hadn't realized that she'd been tense and worried about it until after she and her mother had climbed into their buggy and left.

Why should I care whether or not I see Isaac Lapp? She was over him. Completely. She'd moved on. But the memory of her past feelings for him lingered.

She turned her thoughts to the clinic. She didn't want to wait months until she visited the clinic, especially since her father had agreed to let her go. There must be someone who would be allowed to go. What about Barbara Zook? She'd have to think about it. Barbara was slightly older than her. There were other girls her age in her community. She had to think of one she could trust with her desire to work for the Westmore Clinic.

Isaac took off his black-banded straw hat and ran a hand through his light brown hair. It had been a good workday but he was tired. He glanced over at his younger brother Daniel and felt his lips curve upward. He wasn't as tired as Daniel. This was Daniel's first job on a construction site, and while he did hard work on the farm, he was clearly exhausted from the unaccustomed manual labor.

"Ready to go?" he asked his brother.

To his surprise, Daniel grinned at him. "*Gut* day, *ja*?"

Isaac stared at him, feeling astonished. "You like the work."

"*Ja*. Feels *gut* to see what you've accomplished in a day." Daniel glanced at the house that was currently under construction.

They had put together and set into place all the walls of the first floor of a house. It would be a large dwelling. The first floor alone was probably two thousand square feet. Isaac didn't know what the upper level would entail yet, but he was sure when the structure was done, it would be massive.

"Nice job," Matt Rhoades said as he approached with their older brother Jed.

Isaac gave a silent nod but Daniel was more effusive. "We got a lot done today."

Matt looked pleased by the boy's obvious enjoyment. Dark haired with dark eyes and a quick smile, the contractor was a favorite *Englisher* among their Amish community. "Ready to return tomorrow?"

Daniel nodded vigorously, and Isaac couldn't help but chuckle at the boy's enthusiasm.

"We should make sure that *Dat* doesn't need us on the farm tomorrow." Isaac watched Daniel's face fall. "I doubt he does, though." He made a decision, hoping that his father would agree. "We'll be here," he told Matt. "Eight o'clock sharp, as usual. Let's go home, Daniel."

As he drove their wagon home, Isaac thought of the money he'd earned today, which was his, free and clear. Until this week, everything he'd made since the Whittier's Store incident, he'd given to Bob Whittier to pay for the damages. The paint that had been splattered over the back of the building had ruined the siding. Since there was no match for the old color, all of it had been removed from the building and replaced. And Isaac had paid for it all— the material and the labor to install it—even though he wasn't the one who had been responsible for the damage.

I may as well have been, he thought. Because he'd lied when he'd taken the blame. Nancy had begged him not to tell. Her brother, Brad, had instigated the act, and she'd pleaded with him. Isaac had arrived on the scene after the deed had been done, and as he'd stared at the damage with a sick feeling of dread, the police had pulled up to the building in their cruiser and everyone had scattered into the wind, except for Isaac. Sergeant Thomas Martin, the police officer who'd questioned him, was Rick Martin's brother. Rick was a friend and neighbor, and because of Rick's connection, the officer had called Bob Whittier rather than taking him to the station immediately. Bob had refused to press charges. The officer could have pressed charges himself, but he'd let Bob handle the situation himself. Bob Whittier had said that he'd forget about the incident if Isaac would pay for the damages. So for the next couple of years, Isaac had worked hard and paid Bob Whittier every cent he'd earned until the debt was paid. He'd given Bob the last payment owed with his last paycheck.

"Isaac," Daniel said, pulling Isaac from his dark thoughts. "I did all right today, *ja*?"

Isaac nodded. "You did fine, *Bruder*."

His brother appeared relieved. "*Danki* for getting me the job."

He ran a weary hand across the back of his neck before he turned toward his brother. "You're a *gut* worker. Matt asked if I knew anyone and I did—you. Jed agreed that you were the man for the job."

Daniel looked pleased that both brothers had approved of him. "I appreciate it."

Isaac studied him. Daniel wore a blue shirt, triblend denim pants and heavy work boots, just like he did. His straw hat sat crookedly on his head. There was a smudge of dirt across one cheek and sawdust on the shirtfront, but he looked happy and content and that was all that mattered. He wondered what his mother would say when she saw them. "We'd better clean up outside before we head into the house. *Mam* is bound to take one look at us and cry out. But you can't work and stay clean, too, *ja*?"

"Ja," Daniel agreed with a grin.

They headed toward the back of the house. As they passed an open window, Isaac heard his mother's voice. "Isaac, Daniel—that you?"

"Ja, Mam," they both answered.

"Just stopping to wash up at the pump."

"Hannah," he heard *Mam* call. "Get your *bruders* some soap and towels. They're outside."

Isaac heard his little sister murmur her assent as he pumped the handle that set forth a gush of water. "You first," he told Daniel.

His younger brother reached in and cupped his hands full of cold water, then splashed his face and neck."

Hannah appeared and handed him soap. Isaac stood by watching as Daniel lathered up his face, neck, arms and hands while Hannah hovered nearby, waiting with a towel. Meeting his little sister's gaze, Isaac grinned at her.

Daniel finished up, and then Isaac took his turn. He washed up while his brother worked the pump and his sister looked on.

"You boys done yet?" *Mam* called out. "I need you to do something for me."

"Coming," Isaac replied.

As the three siblings approached the back door that led to the kitchen, Isaac put a hand on his sister's shoulder. "Did you have a *gut* day, Hannah?"

"Ja, I got to play with Susanna. Joseph helped with EJ." She beamed up at him. "Annie came to *Mam's* quilting bee today."

Isaac nodded as he reached to open the door and waited for Daniel and Hannah to precede him. Hannah hung back as Daniel went in first. She seemed eager to talk about the day. "*Ja*, and Mae, Nancy and Charlotte came—so did Josie and Ellen," she went on. "And Elizabeth and her *mudder*, too."

"That's nice," he said. Isaac felt his belly warm at the mention of Ellen. Since her accident, he hadn't been able to get her out of his mind. Or was it because he was bothered that she'd seemed to go out of her way to avoid him since?

Mam was at the kitchen sink, washing dishes. She turned as they entered. "*Gut.*" She eyed him and Daniel, assessing their appearance. "You look clean enough," she decided.

Isaac glanced at her with raised eyebrows. "You need us for something?"

She dried her hands on a tea towel and laid it to dry over the end of the dish rack. "*Ja.* I'd like you to carry my quilt frame upstairs. Martha may stop by at any time, and I don't want her to see the baby quilt before it's done and we're ready to give it to her."

"In the sewing room," Isaac guessed.

"*Ja*, it should fit if you set it against the far wall without blocking my sewing machine." She watched approvingly as Daniel grabbed one end of the rack while Isaac picked up the other. They put it where instructed, and Daniel went back downstairs. Isaac paused a moment to admire the quilt.

Isaac changed his clothes, then returned to the kitchen. He mentioned how beautiful he thought the quilt was.

His mother looked pleased. "I think she'll like it, *ja*?"

Isaac agreed. "You had a *gut* quilting day."

"There were ten of us, and although space around the rack was limited, we worked well together." She had dried the dishes and set them on the counter. She grabbed them again and placed them on the kitchen table.

Daniel returned and appeared to have changed his clothes, as well. *Mam* looked at him, nodded approvingly. "Daniel, will you run these over to the Masts'? Josie needs them." She gestured toward the dishes and bowls on the table.

Isaac felt something shift inside him as he thought of Ellen. "I'll go."

His mother studied him silently but then nodded. Hannah walked into the room.

"I can take Hannah with me." He addressed his sister. "Hannah, would you like to take a ride to the William Masts with me?"

"Ja!" Hannah glanced at *Mam*. "May I?"

Katie's face grew soft. *"Ja*, you may go."

"You don't need me to go, then," Daniel said. "Is there something you want me to do?"

"You can feed the animals."

The boy nodded and left to do the chore.

"Hannah," *Mam* said, "go into the other room and get the scissors and box of straight pins Ellen left behind."

As Hannah ran to do their mother's bidding, *Mam* explained, "Ellen forgot them. I know she'll need them before we can get together again. You can give them to Josie if Ellen isn't home."

His heart skipped a beat. "I will."

He and Hannah headed to the William Mast farm in the family market wagon. It was a clear day, and Isaac enjoyed the colorful countryside as he listened to his sister keep up a running dialogue of what she'd done today and what she planned to do tomorrow.

Chapter Five

"I know why Ellen forgot her pins and scissors," Hannah gushed in between relating other events that had taken place that day.

Isaac regarded his sister with good humor. "Why?"

"'Cause of Elizabeth Troyer," she said as if he'd understand.

"What does Elizabeth have to do with Ellen's forgotten pins? Did she borrow them?"

His adorable little sister made a face. "*Nay, bruder.* Ellen and Elizabeth talked with each other for a time. I know what they said. I could hear them."

He wouldn't ask. It seemed somehow wrong to ask, but Hannah was more than willing to tell, and so Isaac figured he could listen.

"*Rumspringa,*" she said. "Ellen and Elizabeth had planned a trip into Lancaster for meals and shopping, but Elizabeth wasn't allowed to go. I could tell she was disappointed. How old do I have to be before I go *rumspringa*?"

Rumspringa? he thought. *Ellen?* The idea didn't sit well with him. He knew more than anyone else how wrong things could turn in the English world if one wasn't careful. He didn't like the thought of Ellen out and about on her own. *Elizabeth can't go with her.* He breathed a sigh of relief.

"Isaac!" Hannah said sharply, and he realized that she'd been waiting for him to answer.

"Sixteen or seventeen," he said.

"*Ach*, that is a long time from now."

Not long enough, he thought.

The Mast farm loomed ahead. Isaac pulled on the reins enough to slow for the turn and once on the road that led to the farmhouse, he turned to his sister. "Why are you in a hurry to grow up, Hannah? You should enjoy being eight. 'Tis a *gut* age to be." As he pulled into the barnyard to park, he could feel his sister studying him intently. "What's wrong?" he asked, turning to her with a small smile.

"I forgot," she said soberly. "You didn't have a *gut rumspringa*."

His smile faded. "*Nay*, I didn't."

She stared at him, refusing to look away. "She wasn't *gut* for you. Nancy," she clarified. "You need someone better."

His lips twitched. His sister rarely failed to amuse him. "I do? Like who?"

Just then, Ellen Mast exited the house, but she hesitated when she saw their buggy. He could almost feel her stiffen when she realized he was there.

"Ellen," Hannah said.

"*Ja*, that's Ellen." His heart started to thump hard, for he knew he had to find a way to apologize for the way he'd treated her after he'd met Nancy. He'd been thinking about it a lot lately. He should have said he was sorry a long time ago.

"*Nay*. That's not what I meant. I meant that Ellen Mast is the right girl for you."

Startled, he met his sister's gaze. There was a look of maturity in those blue depths that took him aback. "Ellen is a neighbor," he said. *And once a friend.*

"She can be more to you."

He shook his head. "You don't understand how things work between a man and woman."

Hannah's look turned cheeky. "Then 'tis a *gut* thing that you're not a man, nor is Ellen a woman."

"Oh?" He glanced back toward the porch in time to watch Ellen slip back into the house. Her quick exit disturbed him. How could he put things right between them? They'd been friends once. *Now she barely acknowledges me.* "At what age do you consider a boy a man and a girl a woman?" he asked Hannah, wondering with amusement how she would respond.

"A boy and girl become adults when they marry after they join the church," she said with authority.

Isaac could only nod. *She's right*, he thought. Before marriage, a boy and girl would become adult members of the church. In so doing, they'd be accepting the Amish faith and the Lord as the right path for them.

He climbed out of the vehicle with a heavy heart. He didn't know if he would ever join the church. After lying about the Whittier's Store debacle, he felt unworthy of the Lord.

He reached into the buggy to retrieve the dishes and pie plates for Josie. Hannah carried the scissors and pins as she joined him before they approached the house.

He halted. "Hannah, don't say anything about your thoughts to Ellen," he said. "She won't appreciate it."

"Because she is mad at you?"

He released a sharp breath as he struggled with the correct answer. "*Ja*, because she is mad at me."

"You could make her not mad at you," she suggested as they climbed the porch steps and reached the front door.

"Hannah," he warned.

She scowled at him, but good-naturedly. "I won't say anything."

He was so happy to hear her agree that he wanted to hug her. Instead he knocked and waited with a thundering heart for someone to answer.

Ellen's younger brother Elam opened the door and stared at them. Isaac gazed back.

"Elam," Hannah said in an extremely grown-up voice. "Is your *mam* home?"

Elam drew his gaze from Isaac to glance with surprise at the young girl. "Hannah," he murmured with a blush. He turned quickly away. "*Mam!* Someone here to see you!"

Josie appeared from the back of the house, drying her hands on a tea towel. "Isaac. Hannah." She looked at her son with raised eyebrows. "Why haven't you invited them in?"

"Sorry." Elam turned a darker shade of red and stepped aside. "Come in."

"*Mam* asked us to bring these to you," Isaac said as he extended the dishes and pie plates. "She said you'd need them before you visited again."

"And Ellen forgot these," Hannah added, holding up the scissors and pins.

"She did?" A flicker of concern entered Josie's expression before it was gone, as if Ellen's forgetfulness worried her. "Hannah, why don't you bring those upstairs? You know where her room is."

Hannah nodded and flashed him a look before Isaac watched her disappear from view. He then heard her footsteps on the stairs.

"Come into the kitchen, Isaac," Josie invited politely. "I have iced tea and cookies."

"I would enjoy some." Isaac smiled and followed her into the large kitchen at the back of the house.

She knew she shouldn't have disappeared into the house the way she had, but the last thing she wanted was to see or speak with Isaac Lapp. Ellen sat on her bed, annoyed with herself about needing to avoid him. She rose from her mattress and approached the window. The Lapp market wagon was still outside. Why was he here? Surely not to see her.

A knock on her bedroom door gave her a jolt. "Who is it?"

"Hannah Lapp," a muffled young voice said.

Ellen couldn't help her sudden smile. There was something warm and inviting about the youngest Lapp child, the only daughter in Katie and Samuel Lapp's large family household, which included seven sons. "Come in, Hannah."

The door opened immediately and the eight-year-old girl entered the room.

"What brings you here this afternoon, Hannah? Didn't we just see each other?"

Hannah nodded. "We did, but you forgot these." The

girl handed Ellen her sewing scissors and container of straight pins.

Startled, Ellen stared at the precious sewing items in her hand. She'd left her scissors and pins? What could she have been thinking? She used those scissors and pins every day. How on earth could she have left them behind?

"*Danki*, Hannah. I didn't realize I'd left them. I guess I would have known soon enough when I looked for them." She set the scissors and pins on the small table near her bed.

"I found them next to your chair."

"'Twas kind of you to bring them."

Hannah glanced about Ellen's room, noticing the neatly made bed and the slight indent in the quilt covering where Ellen had sat only moments ago.

"You're an only girl like me," she said.

"I am." Ellen murmured her agreement and had an image of Isaac downstairs waiting for his sister.

"You ever share your room?" Hannah asked.

"*Ja*, with my cousin Sarah when she first came to Happiness. Before she and Jedidiah wed."

Hannah regarded her thoughtfully a minute. She approached to where Ellen stood near the window and glanced outside. "I've never shared my room."

Ellen felt sadness radiate off the normally effervescent child. "You can stay with me sometime. I wouldn't mind." She bit her lip, wondering why she'd made the impulsive offer.

Hannah's blue eyes brightened. "*Ja?*"

Ellen felt her reservations vanish. "*Ja.*" Half expecting Hannah to set a date, she was pleasantly surprised when the girl quietly thanked her, then moved toward the door.

"I should go," she said. "Isaac is waiting for me downstairs."

"It was nice to see you again, Hannah. *Danki* for bringing my scissors and pins."

The child grinned. "I knew you'd need them." She lowered her voice to a whisper. "You're a much better quilter than a lot of them."

Ellen chuckled. "I don't know about that."

Hannah eyed her soberly, showing Ellen how serious she was. "I do." She put her hand on the doorknob. "I'll see you on Sunday, Ellen."

Ellen murmured her assent as she followed the child to the door. Hannah stepped through the opening and turned one last time. Something in her expression made Ellen reach out and embrace her. Hannah responded immediately. Placing her arms about Ellen's waist, she hugged back hard.

After Hannah left, Ellen returned to the window, waiting for her and Isaac to exit the house. But when minutes passed and there was no sign of them, Ellen worried about how long she could stay upstairs and avoid Isaac without it appearing strange.

She bit her lip and then firmed her resolve. There was no reason to avoid him. She drew a fortifying breath before she left her room and descended the stairs. As she reached the bottom landing, she heard Isaac's deep masculine voice. She froze as her breath hitched and a burning entered her stomach.

Move, she commanded herself, and she obeyed, entering the kitchen in time to see Isaac raise an iced tea glass to his lips, then swallow his last mouthful. His gaze locked with hers as he slowly lowered the glass.

"Isaac," she said.

"*Hallo*, Ellen."

"I didn't realize I'd left my pins and scissors. *Danki* for bringing them."

A troubled look entered his expression and was gone. As their gazes stayed locked, she saw him visibly relax. "Our pleasure." He turned to his little sister. "Are you ready to go?"

Hannah nodded. "*Danki* for the iced tea. I would have taken a cookie, too, but 'tis almost suppertime, and—" she turned to warmly regard her older brother "—I can't eat as much as he does."

Mam gasped out a laugh, and Ellen couldn't help snickering.

Isaac swung his attention to Ellen. The amusement and good humor in his gray gaze made her think of those earlier times when they'd been good friends. The warmth she'd felt faded as she turned her attention to Hannah, who was tugging on her brother's arm, pulling him toward the door.

Ellen realized that she must have murmured an appropriate goodbye as they left, because they were here one moment and in the next they were gone. She stood, reeling from her encounter with Isaac. She shuddered out a sigh as she headed back to her room. The man still had the power to disturb her. She wondered if she'd ever get over him.

Chapter Six

Saturday—the day she'd hoped to go to Lancaster with Elizabeth—had come and gone. That night, she'd grown sick to her stomach, and the illness, or whatever it was, lasted into the next day. She had stayed home from Sunday services, encouraged to do so by her mother. She'd rested for the entire day, eating a couple of dry crackers for breakfast, then managing a bowl of chicken soup with a few more crackers for lunch. By the time her family had returned home after church services and the midday meal, she had been feeling better. This morning, she woke up back to her normal self.

Since it was Monday, Ellen kept busy doing chores, which included the baking for the week. By late afternoon, she was done in the kitchen and had a few minutes to sit and enjoy a cup of tea before asking what else she could do to help her mother.

"Ellen," her *mam* said as she entered the kitchen. "I just went to the mailbox." She held up a letter. "We're going to have a visitor for a few days. Mary Ruth Fisher, our cousin."

Ellen was unable to place the name. "Have I met her?"

"*Nay,* she is actually my cousin Lizzie's *dochter.* Lizzie wrote a while back and said that the girl has been wonderful but that she's been working too hard. She has six siblings." Her mother paused. "I wrote back and invited Mary Ruth to come." She waved the letter. "Lizzie agreed that it would be *gut* for her daughter to spend time with family."

"How old is she?"

"Seventeen—the same age as you."

Ellen smiled. "I'll enjoy getting to know her. When will she arrive?"

"The day after tomorrow. She lives in Honeysuckle in the northern part of Lancaster County."

"How come she's never visited before?"

"The children have suffered much tragedy in their lives. First their *mudder* passed, then two years later their *vadder.* Lizzie is actually their stepmother."

"And Lizzie takes care of them all?"

"At first she did," *Mam* said. "And then Abraham's younger *bruder* came back to claim the farm. Lizzie had never met him. After Abraham, Lizzie's husband, passed on, Lizzie wrote to Zachariah to inform him of Abe's death. It took a long time for the news to reach the family. Zack's *mudder* had moved them away from the farm after her husband died. The farm rightfully belongs to Zack, the youngest. At first Lizzie was concerned that she'd lose everything—the children she loved like her own and her home."

"What happened?"

Mam smiled as she refolded the letter. "They fell

in love and later married. They are raising Abraham's
seven children together."

"The Lord blessed them," Ellen said.

"*Ja.* He did." *Mam* slipped the letter back into its en-
velope. "Would you see to your room and then help go
through the *haus* to make sure it's presentable?"

Ellen chuckled. "You know it is, but I'll go over it
again if it will make you feel better." *Mam*, with her
help, kept up with the housework. In fact, her chores
before the baking today had included dusting, sweep-
ing all the rooms and cleaning the bathroom.

Finished with her tea, Ellen went through the house,
as promised. It was in good shape, except for Will and
Elam's room. She entered her brothers' bedroom to find
dirty clothes on the floor. She shook her head as she
picked them up, but she really didn't mind. The boys
usually kept their garments on their wall hooks and put
their dirty garments in the laundry basket downstairs.
She held up the shirt and pants for her inspection. Will
must have dressed in a hurry for school this morning
and found dirt, then quickly changed, she realized as
she put the garments outside the room to take on her
way down to the laundry later.

Satisfied that the room was neat, Ellen checked
the rest of the upstairs. Then she retrieved the dirty
garments and headed downstairs. She tossed Will's
things in the washing machine and went in search of
her mother. She found *Mam* outside in her vegetable
garden pulling weeds.

"Everything in the house looks *gut, Mam*," she assured her as she approached. "Do you need anything
from the market? I can go if you'd like."

Despite a pantry filled with food, she knew her mother would want a few special items for Mary Ruth's stay.

"*Ja*, I have a list," her mother said. They entered the house. Ellen followed her mother into the kitchen, where *Mam* gave her the list. "You can get whatever you need in Yoder's General Store."

As she drove the buggy to Yoder's, Ellen felt jumpy whenever she heard a car approach from behind. The memory of those English boys who'd run her off the road was upsetting. The store loomed ahead. Ellen put her battery-operated left blinker on before making the turn. She parked, tied up her horse and went inside.

Margaret Yoder, the owner of the store, was behind the counter as Ellen walked in. "*Hallo*, Margaret," she greeted with a smile.

"Ellen! 'Tis nice to see you. How are your *mudder* and *vadder*?"

"*Gut*. And your family—are they well? I haven't seen Henry in a long time. How is he?"

"He stays busy working in Ephrata—" she came around the counter "—for a cabinetmaker." She smiled. "What can I get for you today?"

Ellen unfolded her mother's shopping list and began to read it aloud. "Flour, sugar, cream of tartar, molasses— Do you have sorghum molasses?" She went on to tell Margaret about her *mam's* other requests.

"*Ja*. How much do you need?"

"One quart jar will be plenty."

Margaret helped Ellen find everything her mother wanted, and after Ellen had paid, the woman assisted by carrying some of the groceries to Ellen's buggy.

"Tell Josie I said *hallo*," Margaret said. "And William."

Ellen nodded. "Give my best to your Henrys." Margaret's son had been named after his father.

"I will." With a little wave, Margaret returned to her store.

Ellen drove out of the parking lot and headed for home. The rear bench in the buggy was filled with grocery bags. She wondered what her mother's plans were for all this food for when Mary Ruth arrived in two days.

Ellen murmured a silent prayer that her ride home would be as uneventful as the trip to Yoder's. When she saw an Amish woman bending over something in the middle of the road, she realized that the ride wasn't meant to be uneventful. She recognized the woman as Nell Stoltzfus, one of Arlin and Missy's five daughters and a cousin to the Lapp siblings. She pulled her buggy over to the side of the road and got out. There was no other buggy in sight, which meant that Nell must have walked here.

Ellen approached, her brow furrowing with concern when Nell looked up with tears in her eyes. "Nell, is something wrong?"

"Thanks be to *Gott*!" She appeared relieved to see her. "This puppy is badly hurt. I was walking home from Aunt Katie's when I saw a car slow ahead. Then someone threw open a door and tossed the dog out of the vehicle while it was still moving. The car sped off in a hurry after that. I saw him hit the ground," she said, gesturing toward the little dog. She sniffed. "He can't get up."

Ellen bent for a closer look. She felt the immediate sting of tears as she saw how the dog was trying valiantly to stand up but couldn't. Every time he tried, he whimpered. One or more of the animal's legs had to be injured. "What can I do to help?"

"Can you take us home—me and the puppy? I'll find someone to help him there."

"I don't know, Nell. I know you're *gut* with animals, but are you sure it's best for him if you try to help him? Maybe we should take him to that new English veterinarian in town—I think his name is James Pierce." Fortunately, there was nothing in her grocery bags that wouldn't keep until after she'd helped Nell. "It might be the best thing for him."

The young woman hesitated, then gave a nod. "I remember seeing a sign for his office, but I don't remember where. Is he far?"

"*Nay*, just past Miller's Store." Ellen studied the puppy, which responded well to Nell's soothing touch. "Can you pick him up or do we need something to carry him in?"

As if God had summoned help, Ellen and Nell heard the sound of horse hooves on pavement as a carriage approached. Ellen turned to see who it was and groaned inwardly. It was Isaac and Daniel Lapp, probably on their way home from work.

Isaac immediately parked the wagon behind Ellen's and got out. "Is everything all right?" he asked, looking concerned.

Ellen met his gaze briefly, then looked away. "Nell has an injured puppy and we've decided to take him to the vet."

"Isaac, *danki* for stopping," Nell said. "Ellen and I were trying to decide how best to move him."

Nell was Isaac's cousin. Her father, Arlin Stoltzfus, was Katie Lapp's older brother. Ellen saw her delight in seeing him and Daniel, who had climbed out of the wagon after Isaac.

Isaac's silence prompted Ellen to glance at him. Isaac appeared thoughtful, as if trying to figure out a way to help. "I have a quilt and a tarp in the wagon. Would one of them help?"

Nell nodded. "*Ja*, either one."

"We've got both in the buggy. *Mam* leaves a quilt under her seat and we've borrowed a tarp from Matt for *Dat* to use."

"Which one?" Daniel asked.

"Ellen," Isaac said, "why don't you take a look with me and help decide?"

Ellen could think of a lot of reasons why she shouldn't follow him to his vehicle, but all of them seemed uncharitable, and if truth be told, there was something about Isaac Lapp that still set her heart racing. She silently followed him to his vehicle, where a folded blue tarp lay in the back of the wagon.

"And there's the quilt," he told her, gesturing toward a folded quilt under the seat. "Ellen?" he said when she remained quiet. "What do you think? Quilt or tarp?"

She met his gaze and saw only genuine interest in her opinion. She softened toward him. "Both would work," she said quietly, "but I like the idea of using the quilt. He's just a puppy and the quilt is soft and can be washed afterward."

His features transformed as he smiled. "Quilt it is, then." He reached past her into the vehicle to retrieve it. As he silently handed it to her, he gazed at her with intense gray eyes. "Are you ever going to forget?" he murmured softly.

Ellen felt a jolt. "I—" She didn't know what to say.

"What do you mean?" But she knew. She had told him she'd forgiven him, but lately she hadn't been acting like it.

His face clouded. "Never mind." And he turned away.

She felt terrible. "Isaac—" He faced her. "I'm sorry. I—" she whispered. Her eyes started to fill, but she blinked quietly to clear them. "I can forget." She never wanted him to guess that she'd been so hurt when he'd withdrawn his friendship or that she'd once hoped to become his sweetheart. Had he guessed?

They stared at each other silently. Ellen struggled with emotion as she saw something shift in Isaac's expression.

"You always seem to be around whenever someone needs help," she said.

His lips curved crookedly. "And that's a bad thing?"

She shook her head. "*Nay*, 'tis a *gut* thing."

His eyes brightened until his effect on her had her quickly suggesting they get back to Nell. Then his gaze seemed to dim.

"Nell is *gut* with animals, but I think in this case it's better if a veterinarian sees the puppy," she said as they headed back to where Nell and Daniel were hunkered near the dog.

"*Ja*, she's always had a special way with them."

Nell sprang up when they approached, Isaac with the quilt. "That's perfect. Now to move him carefully."

"Do you want me to take you?" Isaac asked Nell.

"*Nay*. Ellen's offered. She knows where the clinic is."

Ellen feared that Isaac would change his cousin's mind, but her fears were groundless, as Isaac nodded as if in complete agreement that she should be the one to drive them to the veterinarian.

"Daniel, let's go home."

"But—" Daniel started to object.

"*Mam's* waiting," he said with a quick glance in Ellen's direction.

Ellen couldn't help it: she smiled at him, pleased by his understanding of her need to be involved.

The brothers stayed long enough to help Ellen and Nell gently shift the injured puppy onto the quilt and make sure Nell was safely settled on the front passenger side with the puppy carefully cradled in her lap. Ellen saw Isaac note the groceries on her backseat. She wondered if he might suggest a change in plans but he didn't.

"Ellen, we could take your groceries home for you," he suggested as he came around the vehicle to the driver's side, where she sat.

"There is nothing that won't keep."

"But won't it be better if we stop and tell Josie what you're doing?" he said with a beseeching smile. "We may as well take those bags with us."

She laughed at his persistence. He was right. Her mother would be worried if she took too long to get home. "*Oll recht*, Isaac." She regarded him with amusement. *"Danki."*

He acknowledged her statement with a nod. "Daniel, help me with these."

The brothers had the groceries out of the back of the vehicle in seconds. "Go ahead, *Bruder*. I'll be right with you."

"I can carry them," Daniel said, trying to be helpful.

With good humor, Isaac handed over the rest of the grocery bags and watched with affection as Daniel struggled to carry all of Ellen's purchases to their buggy. Ellen saw Isaac's love for his brother in his gray eyes and her heart melted toward him even more.

Isaac turned and bent close to Ellen as Nell, in her own little world, adjusted the quilt about the dog. *"Danki,"* he whispered into Ellen's ear, "for saying that you'll forget someday." His breath caressed her ear and neck before he drew back, leaving Ellen to feel off-kilter. She was speechless as her gaze followed after him as he smiled, then headed toward his vehicle.

"Isn't the clinic back the other way?" Nell asked when Ellen sat without moving for several long moments.

Jerked from her musings about Isaac Lapp, Ellen nodded and proceeded to look before pulling out onto the road until she found place to turn around. She steered her horse past Yoder's General Store and then Miller's before the veterinary clinic became visible up ahead.

"There it is." Ellen gestured toward a sign that read Pierce Veterinary Clinic.

She worried that Nell might be concerned about the cost of the puppy's veterinary care, but she had money and would insist on paying the entire bill or at least sharing the cost if Nell objected.

"Don't move yet," Ellen instructed after she'd parked in the paved lot near the building. She got out, relieved to see a hitching post, where she tied up Blackie before she went around the vehicle to help Nell. "Why don't you let me hold him until you climb out?"

"Gut idea. *Danki."*

Ellen carefully eased the blanket-wrapped dog from Nell's lap. The animal whimpered as he was moved. "'Tis *oll recht*, little one," Ellen crooned. "Dr. Pierce is going to fix you up. Then Nell's going to take *gut* care of you."

Nell climbed out and Ellen gently placed the dog back into his new owner's arms.

The young woman behind the front desk greeted them as they entered the clinic. Ellen was relieved to find no one else in the waiting room. She listened quietly as Nell explained what had happened and why they'd come.

"Poor baby," the receptionist said as she leaned over the counter to get a closer look. She wore a nametag that read Michelle.

"James!" she called. "Will you come out front, please? Someone needs you!"

Within seconds, a man exited the back of the clinic, a stunningly handsome man with dark hair, dark eyes and a beautiful mouth that went from a smile to a concerned frown as soon as he saw Nell holding the quilt-wrapped puppy.

"Come with me," he urged gently. "What happened?"

Nell explained what she'd seen and Ellen witnessed a tightening of the man's lips as she told him about the way the puppy was tossed out of a moving car.

"Stupid people," Ellen thought she heard the vet mutter.

While she appreciated the man's good looks, she wasn't affected, but Nell, she saw, was reacting differently. The young woman had seemed stunned when Dr. Pierce came in from the back of the clinic. Ellen wondered if Nell silently was questioning the skill and experience of someone who was much younger than she'd expected.

Ellen started to hang back as Nell followed James

Pierce into an exam room until Michelle at the front desk encouraged her to go with them.

Ellen was glad. She would have found it difficult waiting when she wanted to know what was happening inside. She took one of the two seats in the room while Nell settled the puppy onto the exam table and watched as the vet went to work.

Isaac pulled into the barnyard near the William Mast home and climbed out to help his brother carry in Josie's groceries. Shifting his bags, he knocked and William answered the door with Josie standing directly behind him.

"Isaac! Daniel!" Josie exclaimed, moving forward. Her gaze was wary as it glanced off Isaac to center on Daniel.

Disappointed in the reaction he often garnered since the vandalism incident at Whittier's Store for which he was blamed, Isaac spoke up, forcing the couple's attention back on him. "We've brought your groceries. Ellen is helping my cousin Nell." He explained what had happened and where their daughter was. "She didn't want you to worry, so I offered to let you know. She doesn't know how long the vet will take."

"I don't think Ellen will want to leave until she finds out how the puppy is," Daniel added.

William nodded. "*Ja*, she is kindhearted that way," he said. "As is Nell."

Isaac nodded, but William was looking at Daniel while avoiding Isaac's gaze. Isaac tried not to feel hurt but couldn't help it.

"*Danki,*" Josie said. He saw that she was eyeing him thoughtfully, not with censure necessarily but a look that Isaac couldn't read. "If you don't mind carrying the bags into the kitchen," she said, stepping back to invite them inside. He saw William shoot his wife a look and noticed how Josie pretended she didn't see.

Isaac set down the bags on the kitchen table. "Daniel."

Daniel nodded without Isaac's speaking.

"Say *hallo* to your *mam* and *dat*, Daniel," William said to Daniel as if purposely ignoring Isaac.

Pain radiated through his chest as Isaac headed to the front door. He was eager to leave. William's behavior toward him reminded him of how unworthy he was, how he'd messed up and no one would soon forget. Ellen said that she would someday, he thought. The notion gave him hope, although he doubted that Ellen would want to be friends with him again, not with the way her parents felt about him.

He climbed into the buggy, momentarily blinded by his inner turmoil. As Daniel climbed into the other side, Isaac gathered the strength to push the pain aside—again—and drive the rest of the way home.

Chapter Seven

Ellen thought about the wounded puppy as she hung laundry on the clothesline two days later. Dr. Pierce had been optimistic about the dog's recovery. He'd told Nell that the animal's leg wasn't broken but it was severely bruised and sprained. He taped it for support to give Jonas, the name Nell had bestowed on the little dog, time to rest and heal. The veterinarian loaned Nell a kennel to house Jonas and help curb his activities. When the time came for the vet bill, she and Nell were surprised when Dr. Pierce insisted that there was no charge for the visit. Nell started to protest until James Pierce explained to them that he'd just opened his practice. If they would spread the word about his new clinic, that would be more than enough payment for Jonas's care. He then complimented Nell on her inherent animal skills. Nell looked puzzled, probably because he'd seen her with only Jonas and none of her other animals, but Dr. Pierce said he could sense that she had a natural affinity with them simply by the way the puppy responded to her touch and soothing voice.

"Most injured dogs will strike and bite those who

try to help them, whether it's their owner or not. The
fact that you picked up this little guy without incident
tells me a lot. I can tell you like animals and are good
to them." He paused and looked thoughtful. "I have a
proposition for you—I don't want to offend you, but
would you consider working here until I can hire a certified vet tech?" He smiled. "Think about it, Nell..."

"Stoltzfus," Nell supplied, apparently without thought.

"It's only a temporary position, but I could use your
help."

"I don't know," Nell told him. "I'll have to ask. I can't
accept without talking with my family first."

The man had nodded. "I understand, but please let
me know soon. All right?"

Recalling their conversation as she continued to
hang clothes, Ellen wondered whether or not Nell would
accept the vet's job offer. She had a feeling that Nell
wanted to work there but that the young woman was
afraid of her father's disapproval. Ellen understood that
fear of wanting to do something wonderful but being
afraid to ask. It was the way she felt about the medical
clinic...the one she had yet to visit.

Ellen had sensed an attraction between Nell and
James Pierce. Would that be the reason for Nell to turn
down the man's job offer? Or had she only imagined
the tension between Nell and the veterinarian?

She couldn't imagine getting involved with an *Englisher. Look what happened to Isaac.* It would be worse
for Nell, who had already joined the church. If a relationship occurred between her and James, there'd be
only heartbreak for Nell. Their lives were too different—Nell's in the Amish community and Dr. Pierce's
in the English world.

We women must guard our hearts, Ellen thought as her mind filled with the image of Isaac. She scowled as she threw a quilt over the clothesline. It was Katie Lapp's quilt, the one they'd used to carry Jonas. Once she'd brought Nell and Jonas home, she'd offered to wash the quilt and return it to Katie. The young woman had been grateful; she'd seemed to have a lot on her mind. Mostly, Ellen didn't doubt, due to Dr. Pierce's startling job offer.

Ellen knew that there was a good chance she'd encounter Isaac again when she returned his mother's quilt. So what if she did? She'd get the chance to thank him again for his help with Jonas.

She felt an infusion of warmth as she recalled the look on his face when Isaac had asked her if she'd ever forget about the mistake he'd made with their friendship. She allowed herself to wonder briefly how it might feel to have his attention the way Nancy had, to see his gaze light up whenever he laid eyes on her, to have his lips curve up in a smile that suggested she was the only woman for him.

I have to stop this! Such thoughts were dangerous. She couldn't turn back the clock to when their friendship began years ago so that Isaac could choose differently. She'd been hurt badly enough that she'd wondered if she'd ever recover. But she had recovered. But did that mean that she'd gotten over her feelings for him? She closed her eyes. *Nay.* She hugged herself with her arms. Which was all the more reason to keep her distance from him.

As she continued to hang the laundry, Ellen firmed her resolve to be pleasant to Isaac but not let her heart rule her head. She had clipped the last garment on the line when she detected the sound of a car engine and the crunch of tires on the driveway.

"Mam!" Elam cried. "She's here!"

Ellen grinned, knowing that her brother meant Mary Ruth Fisher, her cousin from Honeysuckle, a girl she hadn't known existed until two days ago when *Mam* told her about the visit. She picked up the empty wicker laundry basket and headed toward the side yard. A young woman was getting out of the backseat of a blue car. The driver was near the trunk, pulling out a suitcase, which he then handed to the girl.

"Thank you, Ted," she heard Mary Ruth say warmly. "I appreciate the ride."

"Had to come this way regardless, Mary Ruth. It was no hardship."

Mary Ruth's mouth curved. She said something, but Ellen could hear only her teasing tone. Ted's reply to her appeared to surprise and please Mary Ruth.

"I'll see you then. Thanks again." Mary Ruth watched as the man got into his car and drove away. Only then did she turn and realize that three strangers—Ellen, Elam and *Mam*, who had come out onto the porch—stood waiting to greet her.

"Sorry!" the girl gasped. She approached with a tentative smile. *"Hallo,* I'm—"

Ellen immediately rushed forward to greet her warmly. "Mary Ruth. *Hallo,* I'm your cousin Ellen."

The girl beamed at her. "Ellen, 'tis nice to meet you."

"Mary Ruth!" *Mam* descended the porch steps with Elam trailing behind. "We're so glad you could come for a visit. I'm Josie. I'm—"

Their visitor looked pleased. "You're *Mam's* first cousin."

Ellen reached toward the girl's suitcase. "May I carry your bag?"

"*Danki*, but *nay*. I can handle it. It may look small but if you knew the weight of it, you'd become nervous that I was moving in indefinitely."

Mam eyed the girl approvingly. "You're always welcome to move in and stay."

"*Ja*, Mary Ruth, there are only my two *bruders* and me. There's Elam here—" she gestured toward her younger brother "—and Will, but I have no idea where he is." Ellen glanced toward her mother. "I haven't seen Will all morning."

"He's out with your *vadder*. They went to see Samuel Lapp. Some kind of project or other."

"Come with me," Ellen invited her cousin. "You'll be staying in my room with me."

"Just the two of us?" Mary Ruth seemed pleased. "I've never slept in a room with only one other person, not since I was really little when it was just me and Hannah."

Minutes later Ellen showed Mary Ruth her room. She saw her cousin examine the space with its wooden floors and double bed with quilt coverlet and wall hooks—and wooden chest at the end of the bed.

"Nice," the girl said. "You have a lot of room. My bedroom is this size but there are two beds. Four of us shared the room at one time but not now."

"You don't mind sharing a bed?"

Mary Ruth shook her head. "*Nay*, do you?"

"Not at all," Ellen assured her. She watched as Mary Ruth set her suitcase on the floor in the corner.

"Hungry?" Ellen asked. It was near noon and she was hungry.

"I could eat."

Ellen grinned. "Let's go, then."

It seemed that *Mam* had the same idea, for her mother was putting fresh bread and a plate of ham slices and cold chicken on the table as they entered the kitchen.

"All settled in?"

Mary Ruth nodded. "*Ja.* My suitcase is upstairs." She paused. "*Danki* for having me."

"Our pleasure," *Mam* said.

After lunch the girls went back to their bedroom to chat while Mary Ruth unpacked the few garments she'd brought.

"I thought we could go into Lancaster one day," Ellen said after it occurred to her that her cousin was of an age for *rumspringa.* She didn't have to wait for Elizabeth to go while she had Mary Ruth.

"Into town?" Mary Ruth said.

"*Ja.* A big town. A city. Maybe we could go to a movie. Have you ever been?"

"Rumspringa?" the girl breathed. "*Nay.* With six siblings, there has never been time for running around."

"You've got time now." Ellen wiggled her eyebrows, making her cousin chuckle. "We both do. I'll have a talk with my *mudder* and *vadder. Dat* can hire a car for us. It will probably be our neighbor Rick Martin. He can take us and bring us home."

"Will he stay and wait for us?"

"*Nay*, he'll drop us off and then we'll call him when we want him to pick us up."

Her cousin looked excited. "When?"

"Tomorrow?"

Mary Ruth gasped. "You can arrange it that quickly?"

"*Ja*, why not? As long as *Mam* doesn't have extra

chores for me to do. And if she does, then we'll go the next day."

The girl's eyes gleamed. "It sounds like fun."

"It will be. But first I need to do something. Will you come with me?" Ellen explained about Nell and the injured puppy. "I'd like to see how he's doing. Would you come with me?"

"*Ja*, I'd like to see this little dog."

After explaining about her plan to her mother, Ellen drove the buggy to the Arlin Stoltzfus residence. The short journey gave Mary Ruth a chance to catch a glimpse of their community. "When we are done at Nell's, I have a quilt to return to Nell's aunt Katie."

Meg and Charlie, Nell's younger sisters, were in the yard when Ellen pulled in and parked near the barn. Meg waved as Ellen got out. The two sisters hurried to greet them as Mary Ruth climbed out the other side. "Ellen!"

"*Hallo*, Meg." Ellen beamed at her before turning her attention to her younger sister. "Charlie." She introduced her cousin. "Mary Ruth, Meg and Charlie Stoltzfus—Nell's sisters." She waited as Mary Ruth greeted the two girls. "We've come to check on Jonas. How is he?"

"The puppy?" Charlie asked.

"*Ja*. Where is he? Is Nell with him?"

Meg inclined her head. "They're in the barn. Come and I'll show you."

Ellen waved for Mary Ruth to follow as she and Meg headed toward the barn with Charlie tagging along behind them. She immediately noted changes inside the barn. It had been some time since she'd visited last, and clearly Arlin, the girls' father, had done work to the building's interior. New stables had been constructed along the right side of the structure. There were animals housed there—no doubt brought here by Nell, who always seemed to be adding to her menagerie.

"Nell!" Meg called.

"Over here!"

"Nell," Ellen said, "I came to check on Jonas. I've brought my cousin Mary Ruth with me. She's visiting from up north."

Nell's head popped up over a stable wall as they approached. "Ellen! Come and take a look," Nell said. "He's doing much better."

As she entered the stall, Ellen saw the puppy standing on all four legs—one still bandaged. The animal was wobbly but was managing to stay up.

"Ah...how precious!" Mary Ruth gushed.

The cousins crouched low to pet the puppy, who seemed to relish the attention.

Ellen rose to her feet. "When does he go back to Dr. Pierce?"

"In two weeks."

"Have you thought about his offer?"

Nell shot a quick look behind her toward her sisters, who were within earshot.

"Nay," Nell murmured, obviously hoping her sisters wouldn't hear.

"The work would be interesting," Ellen said softly. She thought about her own desire to help special-needs children. She'd have to confide in Mary Ruth before they headed into Lancaster. Sometime during the visit, she wanted to stop and talk with the clinic doctor.

The cousins spent a half hour talking with Nell and watching Jonas move clumsily about on all four legs until Ellen suddenly realized that it was getting late. They would have just enough time for a brief stop at Katie's before heading home.

"Do you have everything you need for him?" Ellen asked. She'd be more than willing to help out with money or time.

"*Ja.* Dr. Pierce gave me everything I need until it's time for me to take him back."

"He's doing well."

"*Ja*, he is." Nell reached down and picked him up. The puppy didn't seem to mind being held by her. He snuggled against Nell as if he loved every moment in her arms. "Did you return Katie's quilt?"

"We're heading there next."

Satisfied that little Jonas was on the mend, Ellen turned to Mary Ruth. "We should go. I have one more stop to make before we go home."

Isaac couldn't stop thinking about Ellen. She'd given him hope that she would one day forget the pain he'd caused her.

Whenever he saw a buggy on the side of the road, he immediately thought of Ellen and experienced real fear. He had nightmares about Brad and his friends forcing her off the road again. *Is it any wonder I feel the need to protect her still?* He headed toward the barn to check on the animals.

The other day when he and Daniel had stopped to see what was wrong, he'd been so relieved that Ellen was well. He had understood why she and Nell were upset. The poor puppy had been injured through no fault of its own. Who could be so cruel? Brad could.

He went to old Bess's stall, and when she immediately came to lean her head over the side, he rubbed the mare's nose. He was pleased that he'd been able to help Ellen and Nell. He couldn't forget Ellen's smile when he'd given Nell the quilt for her puppy. *If only she'd smile at me all the time, the way she used to.*

The mare responded to his touch, nuzzling against his shoulder. "You like that, Bessie?" he said with a smile. He reached into his pocket and pulled out a carrot he'd snatched from the refrigerator before he'd left the house.

When had it become so important to renew his friendship with Ellen? He certainly hadn't given her much thought after he'd met Nancy. Isaac felt a burning in his stomach as he realized just how much he must have hurt her. They'd been friends, and in his infatuation with Nancy, he'd ignored her completely. He'd been a fool twice over—once when he fell for an *Englisher* and then again when he'd hurt the one person who'd been his true friend and confidante.

He left Bess to check on the other barn animals. He made sure that they all had a full day's worth of water and that certain ones were fed. Then he opened the back barn door to let the horses into the pasture, where their sheep, cows and goats already enjoyed free range. After shutting the barn door behind him, Isaac walked across the pasture toward the front fence. As he unlatched the gate, he noticed a buggy approaching the house on their dirt lane.

He experienced a knee-jerk reaction as the vehicle parked near the barn and he saw the driver. Ellen Mast. The woman he couldn't stop thinking about. And she wasn't alone. There was another girl with her, one he'd never met before.

He hurried to the driver's side of the vehicle before Ellen had a chance to climb out. She was bent over the front seat, reaching for something in the back, her gaze turned away from him. He saw her fingers stretch toward the quilt but she couldn't quite reach it.

"May I get that for you?" he asked softly.

She stiffened and straightened. "If you must."

He smiled. "*Hallo*, Ellen." She blushed and mumbled a greeting as if realizing that she'd been less than friendly. He glanced past toward the other girl inside the vehicle. "Who's this?"

"My cousin Mary Ruth Fisher," she said stiffly. "Mary Ruth, this is Isaac Lapp."

"Isaac," the girl said with a glimmer of interest.

"Mary Ruth." He politely inclined his head. A spark of strong emotion hit him as he transferred his gaze to Ellen. He opened her door. "If you'll step out, I'll get the quilt for you."

She moved out of his way and allowed him to retrieve his mother's quilt.

His lips twitched as he fought back a smile. "I'm sure she'll be happy you've returned it."

He leaned in to smile at Mary Ruth. "Come inside," he invited. "*Mam* will be upset if you don't stop to say *hallo*."

He saw Ellen exchange looks with her cousin. "We have a few minutes. I'd like you to meet Katie," she told Mary Ruth, who then climbed out on the passenger's side.

Daniel exited the house and saw their approach. "Hey, is that Ellen Mast?"

Ellen chuckled. "Who else would be driving my *dat's* buggy?"

Daniel grinned at her before addressing Isaac. "*Dat* wants us to look in on Bess," he said, referring to their mare.

"I just checked on her."

"Oh, *gut*," Daniel said. His attention suddenly focused on Mary Ruth. "Aren't you going to introduce us, Ellen?"

"Daniel, my cousin Mary Ruth. Mary Ruth, Daniel—one of many Lapp *bruders*."

"There are seven of us," Daniel said.

"There are seven of us at home in Honeysuckle," the girl said.

"We have a sister, too. She's the youngest. Hannah is eight." Daniel smiled. "You coming in?"

Ellen nodded. "For a few minutes."

Isaac felt irritated that Ellen was so warm toward his younger brother but was cold to him. He was genuinely sorry he'd hurt her, but he didn't think she'd believe him if he tried to tell her.

Chapter Eight

Ellen followed Daniel with Mary Ruth into the house, conscious of Isaac following. She needed to gather her composure. What did it matter now if he'd chosen Nancy over her? That was two years ago. She should be well past the hurt by now.

There was no one in the kitchen as they stepped into the room.

"Mam!" Isaac called out from behind her. He was close, too close for her peace of mind. *"Mam*, we have company!"

Katie Lapp stepped into the room. "Ellen!" The woman glanced toward her cousin. "And you must be Mary Ruth. Josie told me you were coming. *Willkomm!"* She beamed at them. "I'm glad you could visit. I'm Katie Lapp." She gestured in his direction. "And these two beside you are my *soohns."* She went to the stove and put on the teakettle. "Tea? Or would you like something else to drink?"

"Danki, but *nay,* Katie," Ellen said. "We can't stay long, I'm afraid. *Mam* didn't expect us to be out this late." She bit her lip. "We checked on Nell's puppy before we came here."

"How is Jonas doing?" Isaac asked, curious.

"He's fine," she said too politely. She spoke to Katie. "Dr. Pierce treated his injured leg and put him on an antibiotic."

"Jonas?" *Mam* asked.

"*Ja, Mam.* Nell's new puppy."

Katie's expression was warm. "My niece loves her animals. I've never seen anyone else who has such a way with them."

"She *is* special," Ellen said, drawing his glance. Isaac studied her intently, and she felt her face heat and turned away.

"We put your quilt to *gut* use, Katie, even if you didn't know."

Katie glanced at the elder of her two sons in the room. "Isaac told me when he got home."

Ellen met his gaze with raised eyebrows. "That was kind of him."

His lips curved. "I'm glad I could help."

The girls chatted a few minutes and then left soon after. Isaac walked them as far as the front porch and then watched as the girls climbed into the vehicle. Ellen picked up the leathers and glanced back toward the house. He lifted his hand in farewell. After a slight pause, Ellen raised her hand to return his wave.

"I'll see you on Sunday, Ellen," he called.

She tightened her mouth but nodded, and then with a flick of the reins, she urged her horse forward. She didn't look back as she spoke to Mary Ruth seated next to her, knowing he might be watching her as the buggy continued onto the road and disappeared from view.

Ellen sprang up out of bed, excited. This morning, Mary Ruth and she would be heading into Lancaster for the day. Her parents had given them permission, and her father had arranged for a driver, as he'd promised when she'd first thought that she'd be going with her friend Elizabeth.

"What time is it?" her cousin asked groggily.

"Five." Ellen knew because she usually got up every day at the same time, although yesterday, much to her chagrin, she'd slept a full hour later. Fortunately, *Mam* hadn't scolded her for oversleeping.

Mary Ruth bolted upright. "Time to get up! What should we do first? Feed the animals?" She climbed out of bed and immediately dressed.

"Nay." Ellen grabbed her black apron and tied it over her green dress. "We'll set the table first. I told *Mam* that I'd make breakfast."

As she got ready, Ellen didn't bother with her prayer *kapp.* She'd grab one before their driver came to pick them up at eight thirty. She had plenty of time to get her morning chores done before the driver came.

Ellen enjoyed this time of the early morning, when the birds chirped with their pleasure at the new day. She descended the stairs quietly, then entered the kitchen with Mary Ruth behind her. The two girls immediately went to work.

Mary Ruth took out plates and cups and glasses from a kitchen cabinet. While Mary set the table, Ellen placed a fresh pot of coffee on the stove to perk. While the percolator perked, she retrieved eggs, ham and cheese from the refrigerator and assembled them all into a skillet. She lit the gas oven and when it was hot, she placed the large skillet inside to bake.

"What else do you need me to do?" Mary said.

"There are muffins and biscuits in the pantry—oh,

and I forgot to take out jelly and jam from the refrigerator." Her cousin nodded and left to gather the items.

The scent of ham and eggs had enveloped the kitchen as her father entered the room. "Something smells delicious."

"Dat." Ellen smiled. "Smelled the ham and eggs, *ja*?"

He inclined his head. "So did your *mudder*."

"Her *mudder* what?" *Mam* asked with a smile as she entered the room.

"Smelled breakfast."

"It does smell *gut*." *Mam* took a seat at the kitchen table. "Did you sleep well, Mary Ruth?"

"Like a well-fed baby." Mary Ruth laughed. "Not a newborn—they cry."

"Ja, they do." *Mam* appeared to be indulging in a fond memory.

"Dat, do you know where the boys are?" Ellen asked. "I haven't seen them."

"Outside feeding the animals."

"I would have had time to feed them," Ellen said.

"I know but this is the day of your Lancaster trip—and you've taken care of breakfast, which gave your *mudder* and me a few extra minutes of sleep."

Elam came in through the back door. "Mmm. Breakfast."

Will stepped inside after him. "I smell ham."

Ellen regarded her brothers affectionately before she pulled the hot skillet out of the oven. "Breakfast is ready."

After an enjoyable breakfast with her family, Ellen cleaned up the kitchen with Mary Ruth's help. Then the two girls got ready for their trip into Lancaster.

* * *

Ellen was headed into town. He found out by accident when his friend Jeff Martin told him how William Mast had hired Rick, Jeff's father, to drive the girls into Lancaster. He knew what it meant. Ellen had been eager to go *rumspringa* and now she would finally have her chance.

Isaac frowned. He didn't like the idea of the two girls wandering about the city streets alone. He had a mental image of the day Brad had run Ellen off the road and attempted to bully her. What if someone tried to bother Ellen? Who would be there to help her if not him?

She wasn't alone. Her cousin Mary Ruth was with her, but what good would that do if the girls encountered trouble?

Daniel entered the bedroom. "Isaac, time for work."

"Coming." Isaac sighed. He couldn't help Ellen today. In any event, she and her cousin were probably already on their way. He sent up a silent prayer to the Lord that Ellen and her cousin stayed safe.

As he started work on Matt Rhoades's latest construction project, Isaac wondered how Ellen was managing. He'd been unable to get her out of his mind since he started work. When he asked himself why, he didn't like the answer. When they were friends, he used to think of Ellen as a sister. But Ellen seemed different now. She had matured. He found he liked this mature, spirited version of his former friend. *Maybe too much.* He frowned as he hammered a wooden floorboard into place. He couldn't allow it to happen. He had to put things back into perspective. He wanted to be friends with her again. He wanted nothing more. He stood and stared into space as he dug into his nail bag.

"What's wrong?" Daniel asked.

Isaac blinked and met his brother's gaze. "Nothing."

"You've been quiet, too quiet. Something must be wrong. You haven't given me a word of advice all morning."

Isaac arched his eyebrows. "Isn't that a *gut* thing?"

"It would be if I saw you smile at least once this morning, but you haven't. You've been scowling since I came to get you from your bedroom first thing."

"I have something on my mind."

Lips twitching, Daniel nodded. "What?"

"Nothing for you to concern yourself with," he replied sharply.

The morning dragged on for Isaac as he struggled with his thoughts—and his new feelings for Ellen. He looked around the job site. Their construction crew had accomplished a great deal during the last few days. Maybe he could leave and head into Lancaster.

Isaac sought out his brother just before noon. "I think I'm going to leave for the afternoon…if Matt lets me go. You don't have to come."

Daniel looked relieved. "I'd rather stay." He eyed Isaac quietly. "You're going to take care of your problem." Isaac nodded. *"Gut."*

Isaac approached Matt Rhoades and asked if he could leave work for the day. "I have something I need to do."

Matt studied him, nodded. "Go ahead. Take care of business. Things are going well enough here. You taking Daniel with you?"

"*Nay*, he wants to stay."

"I'll give him a ride," his boss said. "You're off for the afternoon."

"If you're sure it's all right with you."

"It's fine. You'll be back tomorrow." It wasn't a question.

"I will."

"I'll see you then."

After leaving work at noon, Isaac headed right to Jeff Martin's house to see if Jeff could drive him into Lancaster to find Ellen. Jeff was bored and only too happy to take him.

"Why do you want to go?" his friend asked as he drove them into the city.

He explained about Ellen and his concerns for her safety. Jeff looked skeptical but he remained agreeable to Isaac's plan.

Rick Martin had arrived on time at eight thirty. Less than fifteen minutes later, the man had dropped her and Mary Ruth off near Target on Covered Bridge Road.

"What would you like to do first?" Mary Ruth had asked as she checked her surroundings.

At some point, Ellen hoped to locate the clinic that took care of special-needs children. "Want to go into Target?"

"Ja," Mary Ruth said with a grin. "Why not?"

They passed the morning walking down the aisles of Target before moving on to a nearby Starbucks for coffee and tea. Afterward they wandered about the area. They stopped in a local PetSmart to purchase a toy and a bag of treats for Nell's puppy. By that time, the girls laughed after hearing Ellen's stomach growl with hunger. Then they went looking for a place to eat.

The restaurant they chose was empty except for the

workers. They had eaten an early breakfast and so were hungry for lunch at eleven.

"What can I get you?" the girl behind the counter asked. They placed their order and chose a booth near the window where they could eat and enjoy the view outside. Ellen and her cousin grinned at each other, pleased by how their day was going.

"What would you like to do after lunch?" Mary Ruth asked after swallowing a bite of sandwich.

"I'd like to see if I can find the Westmore Clinic," Ellen said. She confessed to Mary Ruth what she wanted to do and her fear that she wouldn't be able to convince her parents, who'd objected when she'd first brought up the subject with them. "I want to stop in and see if someone will talk with me. Maybe if I give my *vadder* more information, he will change his mind. I also need to make sure that the clinic will allow me to volunteer there." Ellen worried her bottom lip with her teeth as she waited for her cousin to react.

Mary Ruth nodded solemnly but seemed to understand. "My stepmother, Lizzie—I call her *Mam* now but I wasn't always so happy to have her as my *mudder*—she has a bad leg. For years she thought she was born with hip dysplasia, a birth defect when there is a problem with the ball of the hip joint slipping from its socket. It turns out she wasn't born with the birth defect at all. She learned that she'd had an accident when she was little and there was permanent damage." The girl smiled, her eyes warming with affection as she talked about her stepmother. It was clear to Ellen how much her cousin loved the older woman. Suddenly, her face dimmed. "Ellen, I think *Mam* is going to have a baby."

Ellen brightened. "That's wonderful!"

But Mary Ruth looked worried. She glanced out the window as if deciding how best to explain. "Uncle Zack is concerned, too. Her hip—it could be a serious problem for her."

Realization dawned, and Ellen regarded her with understanding. "But you'll be happy to have a new *bruder* or *schweschter* if your *mam's* health isn't ill affected. *Ja?*"

Brown eyes shot in her direction as she nodded. Mary Ruth's lips curved up slowly. "We've known each other only a short time but already I feel like you know me."

Ellen shrugged. "You've told me about your family. I know you love them. You would be concerned."

An English family with four children entered the restaurant. A little girl looked at Ellen and Mary Ruth and tugged on her mother's shirt. "Mommy, look! Aren't they one of those people?"

The mother—a woman in her midthirties—followed the direction of her daughter's gaze. She nodded. "Yes, honey, they are Amish people."

The hostess seated the family close to the Amish cousins. The four English children continued to stare at them. A glance at Mary Ruth, and Ellen could tell that her cousin felt as uncomfortable as she did under the family's direct gazes. To her dismay, Ellen was appalled to discover all six family members were now staring at them.

"They won't stop looking at us," Ellen said in Pennsylvania *Deitsch*, the language Amish families spoke at home and within the community. They learned the English language in school so that they could do business with *Englishers*.

"Why do they wear those funny clothes, Daddy?" a

young voice asked. Ellen saw a boy of about six years old and his father studying them with curiosity.

"Because they are different than us."

Ellen stood. "I've had enough."

She studied the food left on Mary Ruth's plate and sat back down. "When you're finished, we can go."

"I've had enough, too." Mary Ruth grimaced. "Let's get out of here."

They left quickly, glad to be away from the English tourists.

"I'm used to seeing tourists here in Lancaster County," Ellen said once the girls were outside. "It never occurred to me that we'd be watched as if on show for them."

"What if we weren't dressed like this?" Mary Ruth asked.

Ellen frowned. "Then they wouldn't stare at us." She knew instantly what her cousin was suggesting. But did they dare dress like the English?

Her cousin nodded. "We could go shopping."

"We could." Ellen gave it some thought. She shrugged. They were on *rumspringa*, after all. "Why not?"

She had second thoughts. *But what if someone sees us dressed in English clothes and tells Mam and Dat?* She'd simply tell her parents the truth—they'd dressed like *Englishers* to keep tourists from staring at them. "We won't be doing anything wrong," Ellen reasoned.

"Exactly." Mary Ruth was studying the businesses in the area. "We could go back to Target."

Ellen grinned. "*Oll recht*. We'll buy clothes in Target."

Less than an hour later, each girl had picked out an outfit. They were conservative by modern English teenagers' standards, but Ellen refused to wear anything too revealing. She chose a modest, midcalf skirt in a pretty blue print with a matching solid blue blouse. She studied her feet while she tried on the outfit and realized that her black shoes and dark stockings would stand out as Amish and clash with her choice of clothes. So she decided to look to purchase a simple pair of black slip-on shoes and panty hose to take the place of the black stockings. While still in the dressing room, Ellen took off her prayer *kapp* and shoved it in the pocket of her new skirt. Pockets were considered fancy in the Amish world but since she was trying to look English, she figured they were allowed this one time. She paid for a large quilted cloth purse to carry her money, Amish clothes, stockings and plain black shoes.

Mary Ruth had chosen a simple green dress. Since it was warm enough outside, she'd chosen a pair of flip-flops. She also purchased a quilted cloth bag for her belongings.

After paying for all of their new items, they hurried outside.

Ellen sighed. "We need a place to get changed."

"Look!" Mary Ruth cried. "A public restroom! We can change in there."

Later, as they left the building with their Amish garments in their new cloth bags, the cousins studied each other's new clothes and grinned.

"Let's see if anyone stares at us," Mary Ruth suggested.

"Let's do." Ellen felt self-conscious as they walked the sidewalk together. When no one paid them any particular attention, she found herself relaxing. "Let's find that clinic," she said.

"Should we take a taxi?"

"*Ja*, that might be best."

They walked to a place where they could call a taxi. Within minutes, the taxi arrived and Ellen climbed in with Mary Ruth following.

"Do you know the Westmore Clinic?" Ellen asked.

"Yes, you want to go there?" the driver said.

"Yes, please." As the car began to move, Ellen spotted an Amish man walking along the road. The figure looked familiar. She froze. She thought he was Isaac Lapp. The thought shook her until she glanced back and realized that the man wasn't Isaac but someone she didn't know. Someone from another church district. She released a sharp breath and scolded herself for imagining things.

Within minutes, the taxi driver had pulled his car up to the curb in front of the medical clinic. Ellen got out first and waited for Mary Ruth to join her. She stared at the clinic sign and felt her heart thunder in her chest. It read Westmore Clinic for Special Children.

"It didn't take long to get here," Ellen said with great satisfaction. "And I think it's closer to home than town."

"Do you want to go in?"

Ellen wanted to, but still she felt hesitant.

"You've come for information and to inquire if they use volunteers," her cousin reminded her. "Dr. Westmore might not even be in today. There's no harm in visiting, is there? How else are you going to convince your parents?"

Ellen nodded. Her cousin had a point. "Let's go in."

The doctor wasn't in when Ellen and Mary Ruth asked to speak with him. The young woman at the front desk wasn't pleasant, a fact that upset Ellen, who worried that she was as rude with the Amish families who came to seek help for their children here.

"May I speak with a nurse?" Ellen asked politely after the receptionist had explained that Dr. Westmore would be out for the rest of the day.

The woman stared at her coldly before she headed toward the back rooms. She was gone a long time before she finally returned with an older woman dressed in white medical scrubs.

"I'm Dr. Westmore's nurse. How can I help you?"

"I'd like to ask about volunteer work."

The woman didn't look annoyed. "We don't use volunteers."

"But I know what you do here," Ellen said, "and I know I can help. Is there a better time for me to speak with Dr. Westmore?"

"Joan, please see if there is room in Dr. Westmore's schedule for—"

"Ellen Mast," Ellen supplied.

"For Miss Mast to see Dr. Westmore."

"Do I have to pay for this appointment?"

The nurse's lips firmed. "We'll schedule close to the time he usually reviews his case notes."

"Oh, but—" Ellen was silently, firmly, handed an appointment card. She sent her cousin a silent message and they hurriedly left. She was disappointed in the lack of friendliness in the clinic staff, but she would keep the appointment with Dr. Westmore. She could only hope that the doctor was friendlier and wouldn't feel the same way.

"What now?" she asked her cousin.

"Let's see what's playing at the movies."

The prospect made Ellen smile.

Chapter Nine

The girls walked to the movie theater. As she reached the theater, Ellen saw posters in the windows and a small marquee listing the movie titles and times. She felt excitement as she and Mary Ruth read the information on the current movies.

"Look at this one! It says it's a comedy, but I wonder if it's really funny," Mary Ruth said.

"The English think differently than us. What if we don't find the movie funny like they do?"

"*Ja*, like the way they laugh when someone gets hurt."

Ellen silently agreed with her cousin. "I wonder what this one is about," she murmured as her gaze went to another title.

"Look what we have here. A couple of lonely females," someone said in a nasty male voice.

Ellen gasped and spun and, to her horror, recognized Brad Smith, the English teenager who'd driven her buggy off the road.

"You!" His eyes gleamed as they raked her from head to toe. "And you've ditched your Amish wear," he accused, looking delighted. "Hey, guys!" He called to the group of male teenagers behind her only a few yards away. "Come and see who's here! It's a couple of Amish girls pretending to be like us." He narrowed his gaze, and Ellen realized what Brad saw—she and Mary Ruth looking vastly different in their conservative outfits from a couple of English teenagers.

His predatory expression gave Ellen chills as Brad continued to stare at her. She felt the hair on her arms rise on end. Her heart began to pound harder and faster as he took several steps closer. She met her cousin's gaze, knowing that Mary Ruth would recognize her fear.

"What do you want, Brad?" she said sharply, displaying more courage than she felt.

"You know my name." The *Englisher* looked delighted as he and his friends moved closer, blocking all avenues of escape. "How?"

She raised her chin. "What does it matter? We weren't bothering you," Ellen said sharply. "Why don't you leave us alone?"

"No can do, sweetheart. I like bothering you." His gaze shifted to Mary Ruth as the other teenagers surrounded them. "You and your *friend*." He smiled darkly as he pinned Mary Ruth with his gaze. "Who are *you*?"

Mary Ruth gazed at him silently, blankly.

"What's the matter with you?" he growled, growing irritated. "Can't you talk?" He sneered. "Are you a dummy?" He laughed as he looked at his friends. "The girl is a dummy."

Mary Ruth scowled. "I can speak. I just don't want to talk with *you*!"

Fury entered Brad's features. His hands clenched

into fists at his sides and Ellen moved instinctively to shield Mary Ruth.

Brad and his friends moved to tightly box them in. Brad flashed Ellen a wicked smile and snickered as he raised his hand as if to strike.

"Get away from her!" a sharp, familiar masculine voice shouted.

Isaac! Ellen sagged with relief as she turned. Isaac approached with Jeff Martin. Both boys were furious. Ellen wondered how the situation would be resolved without a physical fight, which would go against the *Ordnung*, the Amish rules for living. She didn't think Isaac would fight, but she wasn't sure. She'd realized two years ago that she didn't know Isaac as well as she'd thought at one time. On the other hand, Jeff Martin, an *Englisher*, wouldn't be averse to tussling with the troublemakers. But it would be foolish for him to tackle the group alone. The boys outnumbered Jeff five to one. Unless Isaac decided to help Jeff. He certainly looked mad enough to fight.

Brad smirked as he gazed at Isaac. The twisted smile on his lips vanished when he realized that Isaac wasn't alone, that he and Jeff Martin were together. Ellen knew that one look at tall, well-built Jeff, who appeared as if he worked out with weights regularly, had Brad's friends backing away from a fight.

Brad cursed, angered by his cohorts' retreat. Facing the two men alone made Brad retreat a few steps.

"I think we should call the police," Jeff said to Isaac. He pulled his cell out of his pocket, ready to dial.

"Maybe we should," Isaac said, gazing at his ex-girlfriend's brother from beneath lowered lids.

Jeff addressed Brad. "My uncle is a cop. He'll arrest you for threatening and terrorizing young women."

"You can't prove that we did that."

"I'm an eyewitness." Jeff smiled thinly. "I heard what you said. So did Isaac. And the girls' testimony will add weight to what we tell them." His features turned grim. "Besides, I took a photo of you surrounding the girls with my cell phone before we approached."

"No need to get testy," Brad said. "We were just having a little fun."

"I wasn't having fun," Ellen said, able to speak freely now that Isaac had come once again to save her.

"Me neither," Mary Ruth chimed in, but her gaze wasn't on Brad and his friends. Her attention was on Jeff, and the look in her eyes was respect mingled with admiration.

"Fine!" Brad said with a hiss. "We're leaving."

"And you'll stay away from Ellen and Mary Ruth, and anyone Ellen happens to be with in the future," Isaac said with a thin smile.

"Fine." Brad cursed beneath his breath, and Ellen felt her face heat at his choice of words. "I'll leave her alone." He glared at his friends, who waited several yards away. "Let's go," he snapped and Ellen thought she heard him mutter "Cowards" as he left with his minions following him.

Ellen had never been more relieved to see anyone go.

Isaac silently seethed inside as he watched Brad Smith and his friends leave the area. He'd been stunned and more than a little worried when he'd seen Ellen and her cousin surrounded by those thugs. They were nothing more than criminals, he thought.

Why had he ever thought it a good idea to spend time with them? Nancy. He'd done it for Nancy, which had been foolish of him.

He could feel anger rising within his chest and fought it back. But he'd been terrified, and the fear hadn't gone completely away.

It was a good thing that he'd left work early. It was by the grace of God that Jeff had been available and ready to drive him. Isaac gazed at Ellen, and as his lingering fear dissipated, he became angry. She shouldn't have come into town. She didn't need to go on *rumspringa*. He knew she would join the church; he'd always known it. Ellen was happy with her life. So why would she be so foolish as to place her and her cousin in danger? He stared at their clothes. Was it just for the little thrill of pretending to be English? Ellen knew the trouble that had found him at Whittier's Store. She had watched as he'd been drawn in by an English girl and her group of English friends, and he'd suffered because of it. She had tried to warn him. The thought didn't make him feel better. It just confirmed the fact that she should have known better and stayed at home, where she belonged.

He didn't like Ellen's strange clothes. The English garments didn't look right on her. He glanced toward Mary Ruth. They didn't look right on Ellen's cousin, either. He supposed an English girl might find them pretty, but on Ellen and Mary Ruth, the outfits looked ridiculous and wrong.

He glanced in the direction that Brad and his friends had disappeared. He had the strongest urge to walk down the road to make sure that they had left and weren't just hanging around out of sight. If Brad bothered Ellen again, Isaac thought, he would go to the police and confess Brad's part in the Whittier's Store vandalism incident. He could do it without implicating Henry in the crime.

Jeff's voice filtered into his dark thoughts. He was talking with the girls, reassuring them. Isaac looked at Ellen standing next to Jeff, her head cocked a little as she listened intently to what he had to say. As if sensing his study of her, she turned and they locked gazes. A flicker of vulnerability in her blue eyes tore at his insides. He clenched his teeth as he relived the past moments at the movie theater, trying but failing not to imagine what could have happened to Ellen and Mary Ruth if he'd decided to stay and work at the construction site.

"We should go." He addressed the girls: "We'll take you home." He checked with Jeff, who nodded in agreement. They started to head to where Jeff had parked his car down the street. Isaac trailed behind the two girls, who walked with Jeff, one on each side of his friend. He had to work to keep his emotions under control.

Ellen stepped aside and waited for him to catch up. He didn't say anything as she started to walk alongside him. He kept having the mental image of Brad and his friends surrounding her, felt again that awful fear wash over him. He was determined to make sure nothing happened to her in the future—whether or not she liked it.

Chapter Ten

Ellen walked beside Isaac, grateful that he'd saved her. She felt disquieted by his silence. He'd barely said a word since he'd chased Brad and his cohorts away. She'd seen him glance at her English clothes earlier. He looked away when she caught him staring, but not before she glimpsed his scowl. She hated that he wouldn't talk with her. She knew he didn't approve of her clothes and the fact that she'd come to Lancaster, but she'd done nothing wrong. She'd wanted to enjoy the excursion, but mostly, she'd wanted to visit the Westmore Clinic.

"Isaac—" Ellen started to thank him for arriving in the nick of time.

"Not now," Isaac said tersely, and she flinched.

"But—"

He froze in his tracks and turned to glare at her. She gasped as she recognized anger. Irritation. *At me.*

Ellen straightened her spine, started to walk in the opposite direction, then halted. "Mary Ruth!" When her cousin turned, she waved a hand for her cousin to follow. "Let's go."

"Where do ya think you're going?" Isaac said testily.

"To finish our day in town." She narrowed her gaze, daring him to argue with her. She saw Mary Ruth smile at Jeff, then shrug before she left his side to join her.

"*Nay*, you're not," Isaac said. "You're coming home with Jeff and me. Brad and his nasty friends are still out there, and the danger from them is real."

She glared at him, refusing to look away. She fought a battle of wills with him, and she didn't want to give in, but she'd never seen Isaac act this way before. She wasn't sure what he'd do if she continued to incur his wrath.

"Fine, I'll let you!" Turning her attention to Jeff, she said, "I was supposed to call your father for a ride home. Can you let him know that we're with you?"

"Of course." Jeff gave her a slight smile after shooting a puzzled look toward Isaac. He then focused his attention on Mary Ruth. Her cousin glanced at Ellen before heading back to walk with Jeff.

"Are you all right?" Ellen heard Jeff ask Mary Ruth as they continued toward the parking lot and the *Englisher's* car.

Mary Ruth nodded. "I'm all right."

Ellen felt bad as she realized that her cousin was still shaken by their encounter with Brad Smith and his friends. What did he have against the members of the Amish community that made him bully and threaten them?

Jeff pushed a button on his car remote, and Ellen saw lights flash, identifying his car. Wanting to escape Isaac, she went to the other side of the vehicle. She waited as Jeff held open the rear door for Mary Ruth. After her cousin got in and slid to the other side of the seat, Ellen climbed in behind her.

Isaac stood watching, brooding, from a few feet away. After Ellen was in the car, he climbed into the front passenger seat.

She could feel emotions emanating from Isaac in thick waves. She hadn't done anything wrong. Why was he acting as if she had? She firmed her lips. He'd better not tell her father. If he did, *Dat* would never allow her to go into Lancaster on her own, and she'd never be able to keep her appointment at the Westmore Clinic.

Ellen wanted to ask him if he planned to tell, but she was afraid to give him the idea if it hadn't already occurred to him.

Ellen shuddered as she recalled Brad's hand on her arm, the look in his eyes that hinted at his cruel intentions. Chilled suddenly, she hugged herself with her arms.

Isaac looked back, spearing her with his gaze. A sudden heat warmed her body but did nothing for her peace of mind. Face reddening, she lifted her chin defiantly and made a big display of turning toward the window to watch the passing scenery.

The air had grown cool. She glanced ahead quickly and was relieved to discover that Isaac's attention was no longer on her. She heard him murmur something to Jeff. She couldn't make out Jeff's low mumbled answer, either. Mary Ruth had closed her eyes and she leaned her head against the back of the seat.

"Are you all right?" Ellen whispered.

Her cousin opened her eyes and gave her a barely perceptible nod.

"I'm sorry," Ellen whispered.

"Not your fault." Her lips curved into a genuine smile.

"Are you ladies hungry?" Jeff asked.

Ellen spoke without thought. *"Nay."*

Mary Ruth agreed. "I would like a drink, though," she added.

"We'll stop for drinks at a drive-through," Jeff said. "Soda or iced tea?"

"Iced tea—sweet," Mary Ruth replied as she smiled at Jeff through the rearview mirror.

"I'll have the same." Ellen quickly dug a five-dollar bill out of her new cloth bag, extended it toward the front seat. "Here."

Jeff waved his hand as he shook his head. "I've got this."

"But—"

"I'll pay," Isaac interjected, turning to face the back.

"*Nay*, I'll pay. I don't want your money," Ellen said, horrified by the sharpness of her words but unable to help her tone. She saw something painful move in Isaac's expression as her barb hit home and immediately felt sorry.

Jeff stopped at a traffic light, glanced toward Mary Ruth. "I'd like to pay for your drinks if you'll let me." He glanced at Ellen as if to ask permission. "All right?"

Ellen nodded. "Thank you, Jeff."

Isaac remained tensely silent. He didn't say a word as Jeff pulled into the drive-through and bought four sweet iced teas. He stayed quiet as they continued toward home and as Jeff turned onto her family driveway and parked near the front porch of the farmhouse. Eager to escape, Ellen scrambled out of the vehicle.

"Thank you, Jeff," she said softly. She settled her gaze on Isaac and immediately was sorry that things had deteriorated to this harsh tension between them. "Isaac," she murmured and then spun toward the house, fighting tears.

"Thank you, Jeff, Isaac," Mary Ruth said. "I don't know what we would have done if you both hadn't come along."

"I'm glad we did," Isaac said pleasantly. Mary Ruth clearly was not the object of his ire, Ellen realized as she heard him where she waited for her cousin a few feet away. Apparently, he blamed her for what had happened with Brad and his horrible friends. She spun toward the house and hurried to the porch steps.

"Ellen!" Isaac called after her.

She stiffened, stopped but didn't turn. She could hear his approach as his feet crunched against dirt and gravel as she stood on the bottom step.

"Ellen," he said more softly.

The entreaty in his voice had her slowly turning around. She met his gaze and blinked against tears. He made a concerned sound. Something moved in his features before his expression became unreadable. She raised her chin, determined not to be upset if he chose to scold her again. But she ruined her efforts when a tear escaped to roll down her cheek.

His features softened. He stepped closer to her. "I'm glad you are all right."

She nodded, unable to speak. She wouldn't thank him. She wouldn't allow herself to be hurt a second time, although she sensed that his anger had left him.

This sympathetic, concerned side of him stole her breath and squeezed her insides. She wanted to run inside and hide from him. To her shock, Isaac stepped closer and slowly, carefully, trailed a finger along her cheek, tracing the wet trail left by her tear. Stunned, she couldn't move as he tenderly brushed away her tear with his finger.

"I should go," she said, her throat clogged with emotion. Her sudden overwhelming rush of feeling for him terrified her.

He nodded. It seemed as if he wanted to say something but he kept silent.

Ellen shifted her gaze to where Mary Ruth chatted with Jeff Martin, a soft smile on her pretty face. She frowned, worried that her cousin and the *Englisher* appeared to like each other, maybe too much. Jeff Martin was a fine man but he was off-limits to an Amish girl like Mary Ruth.

"Ellen?"

Ellen blinked, turned her attention to Isaac. "I, ah— I've got to go." And she called, "Mary Ruth!"

Mary Ruth glanced in her direction, then said something more to Jeff before hurrying toward the house.

"Danki," Mary Ruth said to Isaac as she joined Ellen.

He smiled warmly and nodded. "You may want to stay close to home."

Mary Ruth took the advice with good humor, while Ellen narrowed her eyes as she stared at him. She wanted to say, "You can't tell me what to do." Although two years ago, she would have been eager to do whatever he wanted; she'd loved him that much.

Ellen turned then, said something she hoped was an appropriate farewell, but she wasn't certain what she had said. Her thoughts were in turmoil as she climbed the steps and went inside.

Isaac walked over to his friend, who waited by the car.

"She all right?" Jeff asked, referring to Ellen, as he opened the driver's-side door.

Isaac shrugged and then got into the vehicle beside him. "I guess so."

Jeff didn't immediately start up the car. "What is it with you and Ellen, anyway? There was definitely something heavy in the air between you two."

"Nothing," Isaac mumbled, worried that it might not be the truth. "We were friends but now we're not."

Jeff raised his eyebrows as he turned the key in the ignition. The car engine roared to life. "What happened? Or is it too personal for me to ask?"

It was personal and Isaac didn't want to tell him, didn't want to admit what he'd done to her in the past and that while he was eager to be friends with her again, he kept doing and saying the wrong things, which made things all go wrong.

"It's okay if you don't want to tell me." Jeff put his car into Reverse and backed up so that he could turn the car around.

"If I tell you, it could ruin our friendship," Isaac muttered.

"I sincerely doubt that," Jeff said, throwing the vehicle into Drive.

Isaac explained about his friendship with Ellen, about meeting Nancy and his infatuation with her. "I allowed my feelings for Nancy to ruin my friendship with Ellen." He told Jeff what happened when Ellen tried to warn him about his girlfriend. He felt something inside him jerk as he suddenly remembered the conversation in startling detail. He hadn't believed Ellen. He'd chosen to believe in Nancy instead. "It didn't take long before I saw Nancy for what she is. I should have suspected, with a brother as mean as Brad." He confided that he'd been distraught over his breakup with Nancy, which she had instigated. He hadn't had anyone close enough to tell. Ellen and he were no longer friends. He hadn't felt as if he could talk with his brothers. He'd suffered alone with his feelings. He couldn't tell Jeff everything; he'd already told him more than he'd ever expected to tell anyone.

"Bad time, man!" Jeff said with sympathy.

Isaac looked at him, understanding that his English friend was surprised and dismayed by Isaac's behavior through that difficult time.

"I've realized that I was a terrible person when Nancy and I were seeing each other." He had just now realized the awful truth.

To his amazement, Jeff laughed. "Dude, you're a guy and guys do dumb stuff sometimes. We're only human." Isaac looked at him. "We are!"

He nodded. "None of my brothers have ever acted that badly."

"Did any one of your brothers fall for someone who wasn't from the Amish community?"

Isaac blinked. "No."

Jeff looked satisfied. "Then cut yourself some slack."

"What?"

"It means to stop punishing yourself. We all mess up occasionally. Forgive yourself and move on."

Jeff must have heard that Whittier's Store had been vandalized and that he had been the one who claimed responsibility. Happiness was too small of a town for him not to have heard what had happened. Yet Jeff had never said a thing about it.

Isaac was silent a long moment. "You've given me something to think about," he admitted.

"Don't wait too long to get a clue, Isaac. You like that girl more than you're willing to admit. Mary Ruth was in danger as well as Ellen, but it's Ellen you're upset with."

"She should have known that it would be dangerous to go out alone."

"She wasn't alone. Mary Ruth was with her. You told me about Nancy and her friend Jessica. Would you have been as worried about Nancy and her friend wandering the streets of downtown Lancaster on their own?"

Isaac felt his skin grow hot and his belly burn. "Nancy is an *Englisher* like you."

"So you think harm won't come to us because we're not Amish?"

Isaac could only shake his head. "No. What makes you think that I was only worried about Ellen?" he asked, afraid to hear what his friend might say.

"Because you like her."

"Yes, we were friends."

Jeff shook his head and flashed Isaac a sad smile as he pulled onto Isaac's road. "You *like* her. Not as friends but as more." He paused. "You've fallen for her."

Isaac felt a jolt. *Nay!* He couldn't love her! But he knew his friend was right, just as he knew he had to fight his feelings to protect Ellen and his heart…but mostly Ellen. He'd already done her harm. He still hadn't made up his mind about whether he'd stay in the Amish community. He knew that someday Ellen would be joining the church happily. She'd stay among the people she'd lived with her entire life. Ellen was worthy of the Amish faith. He wasn't, but Jeff had given him something to contemplate.

If he joined the church and then decided to leave, he would be shunned by his friends and family. He wouldn't be allowed to eat with them, live with them.

He would be isolated, forever punished for his refusal to adhere to his commitment to a way of life laid out by the *Ordnung*.

Struggling with his thoughts, Isaac thanked Jeff for the ride and his help this afternoon. Then, with a heavy heart, he went into the house and upstairs to his room.

He wanted to be Ellen's friend, to make amends for his behavior, for his mistrust of her when she'd told him only the truth of what she'd seen in Nancy. But he couldn't risk making another mistake. He'd have to keep his distance until he could put thoughts into the right perspective about his feelings for Ellen, about his life here in Happiness. He sat on his bed and closed his eyes and offered a prayer to the Lord.

Chapter Eleven

Mary Ruth went home the following day. Ellen was sorry to see her cousin leave.

"I've enjoyed your company," Ellen said. "I hope you'll come again to visit us."

Mary Ruth gave her a slight smile. "I'd like that, but after the baby is born, I will be busy for a while."

"*Ach*, I'm sorry. If there is any way I could help..."

Her cousin widened her smile. "Come and visit. We may not be able to take trips into Lancaster, but I'm sure we'll have some time together."

Ellen nodded. "I could help with your chores...and the baby."

"I'll write and let you know how things are."

"I'll write, too, and tell you what happens at the clinic," Ellen promised her.

"You need to tell your *mam* and *dat* about your visit to the clinic."

A frisson of apprehension ran up Ellen's spine. "I know. I will soon. If Dr. Westmore accepts my offer of volunteer work, I'll have to tell them."

Despite the way of their community, the two girls

hugged. They were in the privacy of Ellen's bedroom. Ellen's family was waiting downstairs. *Mam* had called up to them a few moments ago to tell them that Mary Ruth's ride had arrived.

"I'd better go," Mary Ruth said.

"I'll miss you."

"Not as much as I you."

Ellen eyed her cousin sadly. "But you have a house filled with family—"

"And I love every one of them, but they're not the same age as me, nor do they have as much in common with me as you do." Mary Ruth bit her lip as if wondering if she should say something. "Please thank Jeff again for me. He was…kind."

"I will." Ellen had worried that Jeff and Mary Ruth had felt something immediate for each other. Jeff had offered to take them to Lancaster the next time they went, Mary Ruth had confessed. Ellen had been alarmed when her cousin had told her. But now that Mary Ruth was heading home, there was no reason for concern.

Ellen led the way down the stairs to the main living level of the house. She carried her cousin's suitcase while Mary Ruth descended the steps more slowly.

"I had a wonderful time," she told *Mam*.

Mam regarded her with affection. "We enjoyed having you here."

"I hope we get to see each other again soon."

Her mother smiled. "I'm sure we will now that we know each other so well."

Mary Ruth sniffed. "I'll be busy helping Lizzie after…"

The baby is born, Ellen thought. She saw *Mam* nod and knew she was thinking the same thing.

Dat, Will and Elam had gone outside. They were standing near the car when the three of them exited the house.

Ellen couldn't see whom her father was talking with. *Dat* stepped back as they approached, and Ellen heard Mary Ruth cry, "Uncle Zack!"

Zachariah Fisher, Lizzie's husband and the girl's uncle, had decided to ride with the driver to pick up Mary Ruth.

Zack smiled at his niece's delight as Mary Ruth hurried forward. "You came."

"And why wouldn't I? I've missed my niece and daughter," he said, his voice laced with emotion.

"Ellen," Mary Ruth said. "Come meet my—" she looked up at Zack "—*dat*."

Ellen saw the love between them immediately. "'Tis nice to meet you. I've heard all about you and your family."

Mary stiffened as if she'd just recalled something. "How is Lizzie—? I mean *Mam*."

Zack's expression warmed. "She's well. She's eager to see you again."

"Then we should get going." Mary Ruth turned back to Ellen. *"Danki,"* she whispered, her eyes glistening.

"I'll write," Ellen reminded her.

She brightened. "It was *gut* of you all to have me."

Mam smiled while her *dat* said, "You're *willkomm* here anytime."

As her throat clogged with emotion, Ellen watched as Zack opened the car door for Mary Ruth before he got in beside her.

Ellen heard Mary Ruth cry out with surprised happiness, "Lizzie!"

Mam laughed and so did *Dat*.

"Is Lizzie in the car with them?" Ellen asked.

Her mother inclined her head. "I knew she was coming. She wasn't supposed to, but she insisted. She didn't get out, as she wanted to surprise Mary Ruth."

Ellen saw Mary Ruth wave to her through the back window, saw a pretty red-haired woman lean closer and wave to her, as well.

"Bye!" Ellen called, and then they were driving away and she felt suddenly alone. She couldn't remember ever feeling this way before...except once about two years ago.

"Come, *Dochter*," *Mam* said gently. "We've got things to do. This Sunday is church service and there is baking, cooking and housework to do."

"Housework?" Ellen echoed.

"*Ja*, didn't I tell you? The Zooks were to host, but Peter is ill, so your *dat* offered to have it here instead."

Ellen widened her eyes. "Here? In two days' time?"

Mam laughed. "We'll have help, don't *ya* worry."

"What kind of help? Elam and Will?"

Her mother shook her head. "Here comes our help now." She gestured toward the end of their road, where not one or two but three buggies headed in their direction.

Ellen beamed. It was why she loved her community so much, why the Amish life was the one life that, if she had a choice, she would choose over again.

Katie Lapp pulled her buggy into the yard and parked. While she, Hannah, and their neighbor Mae King and her daughters stepped out from the Lapp vehicle, the two other buggies pulled in and stopped. The second carriage heralded the arrival of Miriam Zook, the one who would have hosted the day if not for her son's illness. She came with her daughters Barbara and Annie, the second sister a Lapp bride. Sarah Lapp, Jedidiah's wife, and Rachel, Noah's wife, came with them. All five of them were eager to pitch in and help ready the house and property. The third vehicle had brought Alta Hershberger, her daughters Sally and Mary, and Charlotte King and two of her daughters, Mary Elizabeth and Rose Ann.

Ellen took one look at the women surrounding her and her mother and realized that she no longer felt lonely. How could she when she was in the presence of such loving family and friends?

Isaac was struggling with his thoughts as he mucked out the stables. He had released the horses into the pasture before he'd started in the stalls. Now he stuck a pitchfork into dirty straw and hefted the forkful into a wheelbarrow.

He couldn't stop thinking about Ellen. He'd acted inappropriately, but he'd been so scared. As soon as he realized that she and Mary Ruth were there at the movie theater surrounded by Brad Smith and his followers, he'd felt a terrible sickening dread. He'd been raised to be Amish. His people didn't believe in fighting but in turning the other cheek as taught in the Bible. But at that moment he'd felt like fighting. He'd wanted to grab every one of those boys and fling them away from Ellen.

Isaac paused a moment and leaned on the handle of his pitchfork. Closing his eyes, he begged the Lord for forgiveness. His feelings, his struggle, made him feel only more unworthy. He prayed that he could be as patient as his father and as kind as his mother. He prayed that he could make a decision about his future that would be best for everyone he loved.

He released an unsteady sigh and went back to work. He'd been horrible to Ellen. He'd let his fears blind him to her feelings. She must have been traumatized and then he'd gone ahead and added to her trauma by scolding and snapping at her. What kind of a man was he? He was neither ready to join the church nor ready to leave his community. He felt an ever-present gnawing pain because he still couldn't figure out what to do.

One thing I can do is to apologize to Ellen, tell her that I didn't mean to be so rude, that I'd been frightened for her, not mad. His anger was at Brad, but he'd taken it out on Ellen.

He recalled what Jeff had inferred, that he liked Ellen, not as a friend but as something more. *Love.* He loved Ellen, but he could never show her how he felt. He wasn't good enough for a nice girl like Ellen. If only he hadn't met Nancy and messed things up, then he might have had a chance with Ellen now. He wouldn't have told a lie to protect his friend. A lie that he couldn't confess to the church elders.

"Isaac." His brother stepped out of the darkness in the barn.

"Eli!" he gasped. "What are you doing here?"

"Just stopped in to see *Dat* for a minute. I'd like to add on to my house and thought he could help."

"I can help," Isaac offered immediately.

Eli regarded him with warmth. "*Danki.* You're a *gut bruder* and man."

Isaac made a sound of dismissal as the image of Ellen resurfaced to the forefront of his mind.

His brother frowned. "What's wrong?"

"Nothing," he mumbled as he stuck the pitchfork into the musty, manure-laced straw. He stopped when he felt a hand on his arm. He looked up at Eli and saw worry and concern in his brother's blue gaze.

"Tell me," Eli ordered.

Isaac shuddered. "I ruined things again."

"Ruined what?"

"Things with Ellen."

"Ellen Mast?"

Isaac nodded. He took off his hat and ran his fingers through his hair before he reseated it. "I yelled at her today." He hesitated. "I made her cry."

His brother released his arm. "What happened?"

Isaac explained about finding Ellen and her cousin surrounded by a group of *Englishers* who were threatening her. "I was scared. If anything had happened to her…"

"You were afraid for her safety. You love her."

"*Nay*, I can't." But, of course, he did.

"'Tis not something you can or can't do. We have no control over our emotions. We don't choose whom we love. God does."

Isaac experienced a fluttering within his chest. "You think the Lord chose Ellen for me?"

"I can't say that. Only time will tell. God gives us gentle hints. How we act on them is up to us."

"And we should do all we can to protect those we love," Isaac murmured.

"*Ja.*"

But he wasn't referring to his reaction after finding Ellen with Brad and his followers. What he meant was that he had to protect her from someone unworthy… himself.

"Stop worrying, Isaac. God has a way of showing us His blessings. He will help you make the right choice when the time comes."

Isaac nodded. "I hope so."

"Need any help?" Eli offered.

"You want to muck out a stall?"

His brother shrugged. "I don't have a stable this size. I don't mind getting my hands dirty for an hour or two."

Isaac beamed at him. "Is Martha angry? What did you do to her?"

"Martha's not angry."

"Oh."

"Let's get to work. I'm sure you have other things you'd rather be doing," Eli said.

He did. But he didn't have a chance of getting Ellen's forgiveness…of convincing her to spend any amount of time with him. He just had to accept that he'd made the biggest mistake of his life and go on from there.

Ellen got ready for church service on Sunday, still reeling from how quickly the house had been cleaned and the cooking and baking done. With so many women to help, it had taken only a couple of hours.

She unpinned and brushed her hair, enjoying the feeling of the nylon bristles against her scalp. Satisfied that her hair had been brushed enough, Ellen rolled and repinned it and then tugged her black prayer *kapp* over her golden tresses.

Today she would see Isaac again. She had been thinking a lot since they'd last parted, about his arrival in the nick of time, his firm stand against the *English-*

ers, his anger afterward. She had come to the realization that he hadn't been angry with her. He'd just been angry at Brad and his friends, at the situation she and Mary Ruth had found themselves in. Once it had been defused, Isaac had needed an outlet and she'd been a handy target.

She felt bad at how she'd reacted, although she understood why. She'd been rude and snippy when she should have been thankful. To be truthful, she'd been more than ready to give him her thanks when he'd startled her into remaining silent when he'd yelled at her.

Later Isaac had called after her as she'd walked away. When she'd faced him, he'd been tender as he wiped away her tears. She might still be upset about the way he'd treated her when Nancy was his girlfriend, but she had to give the man credit. He'd come to her aid twice now. It was only right to apologize, to show her gratitude for what he'd done.

Yesterday she'd spent time in the kitchen baking a pie just for him. She'd made his favorite—a custard pie. She would give it to him today after service with her apology and her thanks.

"Ellen?" *Mam* called up from downstairs.

"Coming!" She knew it was getting late and the community church members would be arriving.

Ellen had dressed in her Sunday best—a light blue garment that her mother had said matched her eyes and made them look bluer. She descended the stairs slowly, anticipation running like wildfire through her veins.

"Our community is arriving for church service," her mother said.

Ellen nodded. With the community women's help, they had cleared the gathering room of all pieces of furniture and in their place sat wooden benches in an arrangement deemed necessary for services by the church elders.

She followed her mother outside onto the front porch, watching as buggy after gray buggy pulled in and parked in a row on the grassy lawn toward the left of the barn.

Ellen saw Preacher Levi Stoltzfus get out from his buggy alone. She frowned, wondering not for the first time what had happened to the budding relationship between the good reverend and Annie Lapp's younger sister Barbara. She hadn't seen Barbara for months until the other day, when she saw hanging laundry in Horseshoe Joe's backyard.

She had to stop wondering about other people's business. She didn't want to end up alone like their resident busybody, Alta Hershberger, Annie and Barbara's aunt.

The Abram Peachys climbed out of the second buggy. Abram came around to assist his wife, Charlotte, who held their daughter Mae Ann. Their other five children jumped out of the driver's side, ribbing each other until their father turned and spoke a quiet word to them.

Ellen stifled a smile as she watched other neighbors and church members alight from their vehicles—all of the Samuel Lapps who resided at home. Isaac, Daniel, Joseph and their sister, Hannah, trailed behind their parents as they approached. Ellen allowed her gaze to rest on Isaac briefly. He stared down at his feet as he walked. As if intuitive, he glanced up, met her gaze, then promptly focused his eyes elsewhere.

Ellen stared at him. *I'm not put off by your behavior, Isaac. By the end of the day, I'll make things at least friendly between us.* As friendly as she dared to be without risking her heart.

"Arlin! Missy," her mother greeted as the couple advanced with their five unmarried daughters. Arlin was Katie Lapp's brother, and Ellen liked him and every member of the Stoltzfus family. She wondered how Nell, the eldest, was making out with her puppy. As she drew near, Nell saw Ellen and headed in her direction.

"Hallo!" Ellen greeted. "How are you making out with Jonas?"

"Gut! He's no longer wearing the cast. Dr. Pierce declared him fit and Jonas has proven him correct, as the little one has been running around the barn, chasing the chickens and digging in *Mam's* flower garden."

"Oh, no!" Ellen exclaimed with a laugh.

Nell smiled. "'Tis all *gut. Dat's* not upset that he chased the chickens. Says they've been easier to manage with Jonas herding them together in the yard. *Mam* claims she didn't like those particular flowers in her garden anyway."

"So they've come to appreciate your puppy," Ellen said.

Nell smiled. *"Ja."*

Nell's other sisters joined them. "What are you talking about?" Meg asked.

"Jonas."

"Ja, what else would they be talking about?" Charlie, the youngest, teased.

"You haven't asked Ellen why church is here today and not at the Zooks?" Leah said.

"Why would Nell want to know about Peter?" Ellen said.

"Peter?" Meg asked. "What about him?

"He's sick. Hadn't you heard? Miriam canceled services at Horseshoe Joe's because of Peter's illness."

"What's wrong with him?" Leah studied her sister Meg's face with mounting curiosity.

"I hadn't heard, and I didn't want to ask," Ellen said, "but it must be serious to change service locations."

"I'm sure he's all right," Meg interjected, but she didn't appear convinced. Ellen thought the girl looked peaked herself. "You're not ill, are you?" she asked Meg.

"Nay."

"She has Reuben Miller on her mind. She saw him recently and he promised to come to tonight's singing."

"I didn't think about the singing," Ellen said.

"That's because we're going to hold it in our barn," Meg said.

"Ja, we thought it would be fun to have it on our property, as we've never held one there before." Charlie seemed eager for tonight's youth gathering. "Are you coming?"

"I don't know," Ellen said. A lot would depend on what happened today with Isaac. If he refused to accept her apology, she wouldn't feel much like going out to have fun. If he did accept it, her attending would have everything to do with him…and only him.

"Look!" Elizabeth Stoltzfus, known as Ellie to her family and the community, pointed out. "They're gathering for service. We'd better go."

Ellen glanced back and saw that Ellie was right. Everyone was heading inside for service.

There was no sign of Isaac or any of the Lapp brothers outside. They must have gone inside. Ellen hurried with the sisters into the house, through the front room and toward the gathering area. People were filling the three areas of benches. Her father and brothers sat on the men's side. Behind them, all of the Lapp men had taken their seats. She tore her gaze away from Isaac to focus on finding a seat with the women.

After everyone was seated, the preacher started the service as usual with a hymn. After two hours of Scripture and sermon interspersed with songs from the *Ausbund*, the book of hymns, the service ended and everyone rose. The women left with their youngest children, while the older girls led their younger siblings outside. The men moved benches in the house to prepare for the midday meal, which would be served as soon as the women could bring in the food.

Ellen disappeared into the kitchen with the women. She pulled items out of the refrigerator and collected other food items that had been placed in the pantry and the back room. She took a quick peek into the gathering room, where men had finishing rearranging the church benches to form tables and seats. Ellen looked for Isaac and thought she detected him in the back of the room. She wondered how she would find time to give him his pie—and to apologize and say thanks.

The men sat down to eat first—it was the way they did things in their Amish community. While the women ensured that their men were fed, Ellen searched the Lapp table, hoping to make eye contact with Isaac. But Isaac wasn't in the room. Where was he? Should she look for him outside?

She wandered outside to check. All of the buggies were still in the yard. If she were Isaac, where would she go?

She hurried toward the barn and went inside. She heard the deep voice of someone talking to the animals, and Ellen knew she'd found him. She left before he could see her and returned to the back room off the kitchen, where she'd hidden his pie. She felt hot, then cold, a bundle of nerves as she carried her baked gift toward the barn.

She recalled Isaac's tenderness as he brushed away her tears, focused on that emotional moment to give her the strength to enter.

She entered the dark interior, waited a moment for her eyes to adjust to the light. She listened but heard nothing. Had she been wrong? Had she been mistaken when she thought she'd heard a voice just minutes earlier?

Something pulled her in the direction of the horse stalls. She smiled. Isaac was standing by Blackie, rubbing her nose as he spoke to the mare softly, praising her.

Her heart melted as she closed the distance between them. "Isaac." She didn't want to startle him, so she'd spoken quietly. She saw he grew still and tensed up as if listening. She moved closer and called him again. "Isaac."

He spun around, startled. She witnessed everything from gladness to fear in his expression before he closed it off.

"I've brought you a pie—your favorite." She rushed forward with the pie plate. "It's an apology—and a thank-you. You saved me from Brad and his friends, and I was rude and awful to you." She blinked back tears. "I don't know why I acted the way I did."

He appeared stunned. Then his expression softened as she came close enough to place the pie in his hands.

"Custard?" he asked. A smile hovered on his lips, giving her encouragement.

Her lips curved as she nodded. "*Ja.* You said it's your favorite." Nerves made her tug on her *kapp* strings, nearly jerking the covering from her head. She removed it instead, worried the fabric with nervous fingers.

"You remembered," he said as if in awe.

She shrugged. "I remember a lot about you." She paused, afraid to go on but then doing so anyway. "We used to be friends."

"*Ja.*" He averted his glance briefly. When he looked back, his gray eyes had darkened. "I should be the one apologizing. I wasn't kind to you the other day."

"*Ja*, you were, actually." She bit her lip. "Before I went inside." She waited for him to speak but he only gazed at the pie quietly as if he was still trying to take in the fact that she'd made it for him. "Will you accept my apology?" she asked.

He was silent a long moment that made her nervous. "*Nay*, because you have nothing to be sorry for. I, on the other hand, should be the one apologizing."

"We could both say we're sorry and leave it at that," she suggested.

Isaac blinked as if stunned. "*Ja?*"

"*Ja.*"

He sighed. "Does this mean we can try to be friends again?"

"We can try." But she was afraid. Could she trust him not to hurt her again? He wouldn't, she thought, if she kept things strictly friendly and nothing more.

Isaac seemed pleased. "We'll take it slow. See how we do." He was grinning as he said it, but there was something in his gaze that gave Ellen pause.

He stared at his pie, raised an edge of the plastic

covering and took a sniff. "Smells wonderful. Will you share it with me?"

"I'll get us some plates and forks."

"Why?" he asked, and the mischievous look in his gray eyes made her chuckle. "Use your fingers and dig in." He held out the pie to her.

Ellen hesitated before inserting her fingers to grab a handful of topping, custard filling and piecrust. She bought it to her lips and tasted it. "It's not the best."

Isaac frowned and dipped in for his own taste. He ate it slowly. "What are you talking about? It tastes *gut*."

Ellen laughed, delight washing over her in huge waves. "You're the better judge. I have to be modest. I made it."

He studied her with warmth. "And for that I am grateful."

She nodded.

"Are you going to the singing tonight?" he asked.

"I hadn't thought to go."

"Want to meet me instead?"

Her heart skipped a beat. "Where?"

"The swings near the *schuulhaus*? I'll come for you. It's too far for you to go alone." He stared at her while he waited for her answer. "Well?"

She made a quick decision. "*Oll recht*, I'll go with you to the swings."

Isaac grinned, and Ellen felt good inside. "One step at a time, Ellen, and we may be friends again."

She nodded and then left to rejoin the others inside the house, but her thoughts remained with Isaac, who stayed behind in the barn.

Chapter Twelve

It was dark outside when, with flashlight in hand, Ellen tiptoed down the stairs of her family farmhouse and slipped out the front door.

The night was warm but not overly so. The stars shone in a midnight sky and the moon was a white crescent hovering above her. She wondered if Isaac would come or if he would change his mind at the last minute. She stepped off the front porch into the stillness of the night and worried that she'd have to return without spending any time in Isaac's company. She worried that she was foolish for spending time with him.

"Isaac?" She walked into the center of the yard.

"Ellen." He stepped out from behind a large bush and into the glow from her flashlight. He looked handsome, and her heart leaped. He'd kept his word, she thought, overcome with joy.

He moved forward as she approached. "You're here," she said.

"*Ja*. And why wouldn't I be?" His gray eyes sparkled in the night.

"I…" she began. "Are you ready to go?"

"I've been thinking," Isaac said. A whinny drew her attention to where he'd parked his buggy near the barn. "Why don't we just stay and walk? The swings are too far and we'd have to come back sooner, but here—" she saw his flash of teeth in the darkness "—we can take our time."

She nodded, relieved. "I don't mind staying."

He bobbed his head. "*Gut.* Let's go." He started toward her father's fields. "I finished your pie."

She gasped out her delight. "All of it?" But she knew the answer before he spoke.

"What do you think?"

"I think you liked my pie."

"*Ja*, I did."

They strolled along the width of the barn through an opening in the fence and kept going. All the animals were in for the night, so there wasn't any danger that they'd escape if they forgot to shut and lock the gate. Isaac closed and latched it, however, before they continued along the edge of the pasture and slipped out a second gate to the outside perimeter.

Walking beside Isaac in the darkness felt awkward to Ellen but wonderful at the same time. It had been a long while since they'd spent any amount of time together, and even longer since they'd been alone. Isaac didn't say a word, and Ellen wondered if he was feeling strange, too.

They made their way along the outside of the fence to the wooden bench that Ellen's father had built for his parents when they'd been alive.

Her grandfather liked to observe the animals in the pasture, and later, when he got too old to farm, he enjoyed watching the workers in the fields. Ellen as a young child had seen the sadness in his eyes and had thought he might have wanted to join *Dat* in the fields. But he'd been able to look, at least, if he wanted and he'd seemed to take comfort in that.

Ellen sat on the bench and Isaac settled down next to her.

"Do you remember when we came here to watch the lunar eclipse?" he asked.

Ellen smiled, recalling the occasion well. They had heard about the eclipse from Bob Whittier. They had both slipped out in the middle of the night to watch it. She and Isaac had talked about everything under the sun as they waited and watched as the Earth slipped between the moon and the sun, casting its shadow to turn the moon a bloodred color.

The memory gave Ellen pause as she felt herself relax. She was enjoying his company too much. She shouldn't have agreed to their meeting. Secret rendezvous were reserved for couples who were courting. She and Isaac were only friends...and friends who had been estranged. Was it wise to try to fix their friendship? After all that had happened, she'd be foolish to spend time with a man who had chosen to believe someone else over her. Could it happen again?

"Did you have any trouble getting away?" she asked politely as she clicked off her flashlight to save the batteries. An intimacy surrounded them, scaring her, and she immediately turned on the light again.

"Daniel went to the singing with John King. *Mam, Dat* and the others went to bed." Isaac shifted on the bench beside her. "*Nay*, it wasn't hard to slip away."

She saw Isaac staring straight ahead in the lamplight. His expression was unreadable. Ellen sensed that something was bothering him. Should she ask him what it was? She was afraid to ask. Did he regret meeting her?

She bit her lip as she studied him. He turned then and stared. She blinked. He'd always been a handsome boy but now as a man, he was devastating in his good looks.

Ellen felt a sliver of dread rise its way up from her midsection. She shouldn't notice such things about him. The fact that she did notice upset her. It had been a mistake to meet him.

"Isaac," she whispered when his eyes rose as if to study the moon and stars in the dark sky. "This may not be a *gut* idea—meeting like this."

He flinched but quickly got himself under control. "You may be right," he agreed too readily. But Ellen heard something in his voice that told her that something else was going on with him. Had he come to confide in her? Did he miss the way they used to talk?

She had known him well enough back then to still recognize the little changes in his expression.

"You are quiet," she improvised.

He smiled at her, a soft gentle twist of his lips. "It's peaceful out here. I was just enjoying the night."

"*Ja*, the night silence. I like this time of day, when we can enjoy the world around us as the Lord intended."

Isaac dipped his head in agreement. He paused. "Ellen, *danki* for letting me come. I know things became difficult because of me. I want you to know that I am genuinely sorry."

Ellen was silent for a long moment. "For what?" She pulled off her prayer *kapp* and placed it in her lap. For what had happened the other day? Or two years ago? She waited for him to continue.

He beamed at her, his gray eyes suddenly bright in

the darkness. "We used to talk about everything, didn't we?" he said, changing the subject.

Ellen nodded. "Most everything," she agreed.

He arched an eyebrow. "Not everything?"

"Nay."

Tension cropped up between them. Ellen was hurt by it, but she didn't know how to ease the strain. The last time she'd attempted to speak to him frankly, he had ended their friendship. She tensed and stood. "I should get inside. I…have to get up early."

He froze. "I see." He got up more slowly. They silently walked back the way they'd come, stopping in the barnyard.

Isaac looked at her without expression. *"Guten nacht."* Then he turned and left her. And Ellen watched him go with tears in her eyes.

It was for the best that he'd left, for she was afraid that she wouldn't be able to control her emotions while he was around.

She heard him urge his horse forward and the sound of the animal's hooves. After Isaac's departure, Ellen returned to the house and went up to her room, glad that she was the only daughter in the house, for tonight she wanted nothing more than to be alone…and cry.

His emotions were all over the place as Isaac steered old Bess home. He'd known that he shouldn't have come to see Ellen, known the moment he'd asked her to meet him that it was a foolish thing to do.

He could still see her face when she'd called for him. She'd seemed almost happy to see him. Her blue eyes glistened in the lamplight. She looked beautiful with the sweet curve of her lips and her pert little nose. Earlier, when she'd brought him the pie, he'd been over-whelmed. Ever since his discussion with Jeff, and then later with his brother Eli, he'd been overly aware of the depth of his feelings for Ellen. But he'd also been over-whelmingly certain that he should keep his distance, yet here he was, heading home after meeting her in se-cret. And Ellen must have felt the wrongness of it, too, for she'd abruptly put an end to their evening together when it had barely begun.

He understood that he'd hurt her. She'd been his friend and she'd been honest about Nancy, and he'd been shocked and too angry to listen to her. Not only did he not listen but he'd avoided her after that…at church and other community gatherings. What kind of man did that to a friend?

The road at this time of night was unusually quiet. He was ever alert for cars. They tended to race by in the darkness and the drivers could easily miss seeing an Amish buggy driver, even when the vehicle was lit up with its battery-operated lights.

Daniel would be at the singing at their *onkel* Arlin's house. Normally, the youth gathering would have been held at the Masts' residence since the event usually took place wherever church services were hosted that morn-ing. But William and Josie had hosted because another family couldn't at the last moment. His aunt and uncle had offered to have the singing at their house so that the Masts wouldn't be burdened with two last-minute unplanned events.

Should he go to the singing or head home? Home, he decided. He didn't feel like having fun. He'd been enjoy-ing himself with Ellen until she'd called an abrupt halt to the evening. He should have talked with her, asked her what was wrong, but he'd been hurt.

He frowned. He could only imagine how she'd felt years ago. Perhaps she'd been worried that he'd hurt her again like he had the last time.

He had to talk with her. He could turn back now, but she would have gone to her room, and with her parents at home, he couldn't try to wake her and ask her to come outside to talk.

I should let it go. Forget about her. But he couldn't. His every waking moment was filled with thoughts of Ellen. He should have realized what he had with their friendship. They'd been good friends. Why hadn't he listened to her? Why hadn't he fallen for her instead of Nancy? Why had it taken him so long to discover that he loved her more than anything?

There had to be something he could do. But he didn't know what. The Lord was trying to tell him something. He wasn't sure how he was going to resolve things in his life. He wanted his sin to be forgiven. He wanted to court Ellen, but until he could figure out how, he'd keep his distance…and hope that he wouldn't lose her forever.

Ellen sat in the silence of her room and cried silent tears. What had she done? She had a chance of mending fences with Isaac but she'd become frightened and sent him away. So he'd hurt her years ago and she'd felt devastated. But he'd shown her that he was someone she could rely on to get her out of a difficult situation. He'd appeared whenever she needed him. That was something, wasn't it? But if he valued their friendship, why had he been so quick to leave?

She lay back on her bed, staring at the window glass where, if she looked hard enough, she could detect a track of moonlight on the white curtains.

Her appointment at the Westmore Clinic was in a few days. She needed to focus on her meeting with Dr. Westmore, be prepared to convince him that an Amish volunteer would be beneficial to his patients and their families as well as a help to him. The appointment card that Joan at the front desk had given her was tucked under her mattress. Ellen sat up, ran her hand under the mattress and located the card. She grabbed a flashlight she kept nearby in case she had to get up in the middle of the night. Shining the beam on the card, she noted the time that the receptionist had scheduled for her. Her appointment was for noon. She had to go, but what would she tell her parents? That she had to run an errand—that wouldn't be a lie. And she could tell them that she would be visiting Caleb and Rebekka Yoder. She wanted to see them after her appointment, so that afternoon would be the perfect time to stop by.

She would be driving alone, but the clinic wasn't far. She'd be fine. No one would bother her. Brad and his friends had been threatened with arrest. Surely they'd ignore her if they saw her out and about on her own.

Ellen tucked the card under the other pillow on her double bed. Then she lay back and tried to relax so she could get a restful night's sleep. She saw the mental image of Isaac's face, his smile…his concern…his anger…his tenderness.

She kept her eyes tightly closed but it didn't prevent the tears that flowed as she thought of Isaac's leaving this evening, the way she'd sent him away. She said a prayer that all would go well the next day—that she would visit the clinic and get an offer of a volunteer job—and she prayed that Isaac would find happiness again. And she couldn't help praying for the strength to accept whatever happened between her and Isaac.

Chapter Thirteen

The next morning Ellen told her mother that she was going to run some errands. When *Mam* asked where she was going, she told them about her planned visit to Rebekka and Caleb Yoder. She also mentioned that the Yoders had been taking their daughter, Alice, to the Westmore Clinic, and she thought she might stop in and visit sometime.

"Why would you want to do that?" *Dat* asked as he entered the room. He must have overheard what she'd said. They'd had this discussion before and it hadn't gone well.

"Because I'm interested. It's a terrible thing what Rebekka and Caleb's daughter, Alice, has to go through as treatment for her problem. It's awful what the Yoders are going through, what all Amish families have to go through when they have children who are sick."

"You haven't given up the notion of working there," her father accused.

"What's wrong with that? If I can make things a little easier for the families and patients—"

"You're not a trained medical professional," *Mam*

quietly pointed out. Unlike her father, who was dead set against the idea, her mother kept her expression neutral and her thoughts to herself. She wouldn't go against her father, but she seemed interested in learning more.

"The Westmore Clinic is on Old Philadelphia Pike, just a short distance away. Dr. Westmore, the English doctor there, treats only children of Amish couples. He's a geneticist who has dedicated his life to discovering ways to help his patients."

"You want to work for an *Englisher*?"

"I want to volunteer. One or two days a week at most. There are women within our community who work for the English. Ellie Stoltzfus cleans for an English family. Mary Elizabeth Peachy works at a fabric store."

"I don't like it," *Dat* groused. "God will take care of these children, not you. You, *Dochter*, should worry about finding a husband and having children."

"I'm too young to marry!" she exclaimed. She immediately softened her tone. "I'm sorry. I promise that I will join the church, marry and have children, but not right away. This is some things I would like to do first."

"I think you should get on with your chores and forget about this nonsense," her father insisted.

"*Dat*, just let me get some information," she began. "Please don't say *nay* before you know all the facts…" She went silent as she locked gazes with her mother. With tears in her eyes, she left the kitchen, where her mother and father were finishing their breakfast. Her thoughts were in turmoil as she went out to feed the chickens. Seeing the hens gobbling up their food gave her no pleasure. She didn't feel amused, as she usually did, by Red, the rooster, when he strutted out of the pen last like a king surveying his underlings. She was too blinded by tears to enjoy anything.

I will find a way. Her appointment with the clinic doctor was in two days. Her father hadn't said that she couldn't go. Of course, he didn't know about her appointment. She would keep it and get any information that might help to convince her father. If he still wouldn't allow her to work there afterward, then she would have to obey, but she wouldn't be happy.

Isaac worked beside Jedidiah to secure the four-by-eight aspenite wall sheets onto two-by-four studs. He was quiet as he hammered nails around the perimeter of the aspenite and along each stud.

"What's wrong?" his brother asked after a time.

"Nothing," Isaac said. "Why would you think something's wrong?"

"You're too quiet today."

A smile hovered on Isaac's mouth. "And that's a problem for you?"

Jedidiah grinned. "I shouldn't be complaining."

"*Ja,* you shouldn't." Isaac grabbed a nail from his leather tool bag and pounded it into place. "I've just been thinking."

"About?" Jedidiah regarded him with a serious expression.

"A lot of things. The bad choices I made in the past. The future."

"You can't do anything about the past," Jed said. He paused. "What about the future?"

He shrugged. "I'm not sure what I'll be doing."

"As if we know ahead of time," Jed murmured drily.

He was silent for a long moment as they continued to work. "Is this about joining the church or marrying?"

"I don't know that I'll join the church," Isaac admitted carefully.

"Why not?" his brother demanded.

"I've done something the Lord wouldn't approve of. I didn't live up to the ways of the *Ordnung*."

"You haven't joined the church yet. So you made a mistake when you defaced Bob's store. You also took responsibility for the act and made restitution."

Isaac didn't agree or answer. "It doesn't feel right."

"You'll change your mind when you find the right woman, someone unlike your former girlfriend, Nancy."

Isaac grabbed one end of a piece of aspenite while Jed grabbed the other end, and the two of them set the board into place. With one hand, Jed hammered a few nails until his side was secure. Then Isaac did the same on his end of the board.

"Falling for Nancy wasn't the smartest thing I've ever done," Isaac said after he'd hammered in a few nails.

Jedidiah finished nailing a board to a two-by-four stud. He then stepped back and eyed their handiwork. "You can't help who you fall in love with, Isaac."

"I could have used better judgment."

Jed shook his head. "As if you had a choice. *Nay*, you didn't plan on liking Nancy. It just happened, and God allowed it for a reason, even if only to show you how wrong someone like her is for you."

"You didn't like her—none of our family did."

"It's not that we didn't like her. We just weren't sure she was the right girl for you. We had hoped for your sake, but we didn't want to see you hurt." He sighed. "And you were hurt—badly."

Isaac nodded as he reached for another nail. *"Ja."*

"Have faith, Isaac. God had plans for you. He will let you know in His own time. I'm sure there is a nice girl for you within our or another Amish community."

But what if I decide to leave? Isaac thought. How would he be fulfilling God's plan then? He couldn't stop the constant struggle within him. He wished he could, that he could simply confess the truth, say he was sorry and all would be right with his life and his world. But he couldn't. It wasn't about only him. It was about Henry Yoder, who had once been a close friend—not in the same way that he and Ellen had been. Henry and he had gone *rumspringa* together. Henry had been with him when he'd met Nancy. And while he was with Nancy, Henry had spent his time with Nancy's friend Jessica, another English girl.

Thoughts of Ellen rose up in his mind. Tomorrow they would spend time together, go for ice cream as they did long ago, before Nancy Smith had entered his life and made a mess of things. He'd sent Ellen a note asking her to come. To his surprise, she'd accepted his invitation as if she wanted them to be friends as much as he did.

He wished he could tell Ellen about what had happened that awful night at Whittier's Store. It wasn't that he didn't trust her, but it wasn't his secret to tell. And despite the fact that he hadn't seen Henry since the night it happened, he wouldn't betray him.

Tomorrow, he thought. *Just focus on one day at a time.* The Lord would help him find his path. Until then he could enjoy Ellen's friendship and work construction beside his oldest brother. Life could be worse. But he hoped that someday it would get better.

The next day Ellen stood at the end of the farm road, waiting for Isaac. Today would be like old times when they'd walked to Whittier's Store together, each ordering their favorite ice cream—mint chocolate chip. She'd been surprised and hopeful when he'd invited her like old times. She looked forward to spending time with him, working toward the friendship they'd had once but lost. Her thoughts switched to her appointment tomorrow with Dr. Westmore. She wished she could talk with someone else besides her parents. Could she talk with Isaac about it? She frowned. Things between them weren't like they were before Nancy. She thought of what she would say to Dr. Westmore. As she rehearsed what she had in mind, she thought of little Alice Yoder and her resolve firmed.

Ellen reached out and tugged a leaf from a tree near the edge of the property. She looked down at the green structure, the veins and edges all arranged beautifully to form the maple leaf. She ran her finger along the surface, tugged on an edge and saw the fragment splinter off to the first vein.

"You look pensive," a male voice said.

"Isaac." She looked up and smiled. "You're late."

His gray eyes gleamed with amusement as he shook his head. "*Nay*, you were early."

Her lips widened as she grinned. "I like ice cream."

"So do I." He reached for her hand and with a little inward gasp, she placed her fingers within his grasp. The warmth of his touch filled her to overflowing. She never would have thought she'd be this glad to spend time with him again. She realized that she had moved past the old hurt and was ready to start anew.

"I wasn't sure if you'd want to walk or take your family buggy," she said conversationally as they began to stroll together in the direction of their destination.

He tugged on her hand, stopped and regarded her with raised eyebrows. "You think me too old to use my legs? When did we ever not walk for ice cream?" There was a twinkle in his gray eyes.

"You may have aged overnight, found it hard to keep up with a young girl such as me."

"Woman," he said softly, making her shiver with pleasure. "There is nothing of the girl in you."

"I think I should be offended." She lifted her chin and looked down her nose at him.

Isaac laughed as he gently squeezed her hand. "You shouldn't be. It was a compliment, not a complaint."

She relaxed. "If you say so." She started to walk again and he fell into step with her. They walked in companionable silence. Ellen started to think about how and if she should tell him about the clinic. Wanting to get it over with, she opened her mouth to start but then promptly closed it. She didn't want to put a damper on the day yet. She'd feel bad if he spoke negatively about her volunteer idea like her father had. Maybe he would understand and encourage her. She wanted his friendship and his understanding of her plans. Maybe she should confide in him after ice cream. Or maybe she shouldn't.

"Do you have to be back at a certain time?" Isaac asked, hoping that she'd say no.

She shook her head. "You?"

"I've got all day." He experienced a wash of excitement and relief that they could spend the entire day together.

It was a perfect day for a walk to Whittier's Store. The warmth of the sun caressed Isaac's skin while a light breeze tousled the loose tendrils of Ellen's blond hair. She was quiet as they strolled down the main road. He chanced a peek at her and saw that her features were relaxed, happy, and he thanked God for these moments with her.

"Look!" she said. He followed the direction of her gaze and saw his cousin Nell with her puppy, Jonas. Isaac watched as Jonas ran around in circles, barking happily, his tail wagging with pleasure as he circled his mistress. "Jonas's leg is healed."

"He's doing well," Isaac murmured, pleased for Nell.

Ellen looked away from Nell to meet his gaze, her features awash with joy. "She's so good with him."

Isaac nodded. "She'd make a good veterinary assistant."

He suddenly felt Ellen stiffen beside him. "You mean that?" she asked carefully, her expression guarded.

"*Ja*, I do." Isaac looked at her with concern. "What is it? What's wrong?"

Ellen seemed as if she suddenly understood him. She relaxed and smiled. "Dr. Pierce offered her a temporary job as his vet tech."

"His assistant?" Isaac asked.

"*Ja*. I think she wants to take it but is afraid."

Isaac frowned as he gazed into Ellen's blue eyes. "Why?"

"Her father—your uncle Arlin."

"She doesn't think he'll approve?"

Ellen nodded. "Fathers often have a different idea of what is right or wrong when it comes to their *dechter*."

Isaac thought of his little sister, Hannah, and knew she was treated differently from him and his brothers, but he couldn't see his father denying Hannah something she wanted to do, not if it meant a lot to her. He knew Hannah was only eight years old, but he still thought his father would allow Hannah to work wherever she wanted as long as it was a place where she would suffer no harm.

"You think your *onkel* would let her work for Dr. Pierce? The man offered her the job until he could find a full-time certified vet tech."

"I don't see why not." Although now that he thought about it, he recalled the way his uncle had become overprotective of his cousin Meg after she'd become ill and stayed in the hospital. He probably would have felt the same if it had been his daughter—if he were married and had a daughter.

"I hope she is allowed to take the position." Ellen appeared wistful as she stared off in the distance.

"Time will tell," he said quietly. He studied Ellen, noting the changes in her features in the last two years. She had lost that baby-face look. Her eyes were large and luminous, her nose perfectly formed. Her mouth was well shaped with full lips. And her chin was slightly pointed but not much. She was quite lovely, but as he'd told her earlier, she was no longer a girl but a woman. And his feelings for her had changed, grown.

She's a friend, he thought, and he had to make sure she stayed his friend.

"I've decided to buy you an ice cream *and* a soda," he said.

She turned to him with a raised eyebrow but with a smile on her lips. His breath hitched. "Why?"

"Why not?" He looked away as she tugged on his heartstrings. He couldn't do it, fall for her and take the risk that he'd hurt her again—and himself in the process.

Suddenly, she stopped, stared at him. "What's wrong?"

He blinked. "Nothing. Why do you ask?"

"You don't seem like yourself." She was quiet a moment. "Are you sorry you asked me to come?"

"Nay."

"You're more quiet, introspective." She paused. "Is there something you want to tell me? I'm a *gut* listener. I'll be happy to help if I can."

He felt something inside him harden. *"Nay.* I'm fine." But he knew he didn't sound or feel fine. Whittier's Store loomed ahead like a lifeline. "We're here!" he announced, and with her hand still in his, he hurried forward at almost a run.

Ellen studied the man at her side and sensed he was troubled. Why wouldn't he tell her what was bothering him? Had coming here for ice cream brought back bad memories for him? Was she afraid of how Bob Whittier would act when he saw him again?

He released her hand to open the door and held it for her. His eyes gleamed at the prospect as if he was eager for their favorite treat. He didn't look upset or pensive. Had she imagined it?

"Isaac," she began as she turned to wait for him, "if you'd rather not be here…if you'd prefer to go to Miller's…"

She felt Isaac stiffen beside her. She touched his arm to offer comfort and felt the tension seep out of him.

"I'm fine with Whittier's," he said, and she realized it was true. He didn't seem upset or look as if he felt awkward.

"Oll recht," she said with a smile. "Since you're buying, I'll have a double-scoop mint chocolate chip cone."

He laughed, and the sound rippled pleasurably down her spine, making her giggle.

"And I suppose the soda needs to be the extra large?"

Ellen wrinkled her nose at him. "*Nay*, a small root beer will be just fine." She was happy to see him beam at her as his gray eyes filled with amusement.

They enjoyed their ice cream, sitting outside in the sun on a park bench. They talked about their families, their farms and the weather. Isaac told her about the current construction job the crew was working on—a large house that was progressing nicely.

"It's being insulated today, which is why I was able to take off today," he told her.

"I'm glad." She thought about telling him about the clinic now, but then she decided not to tell him until she knew whether or not her meeting with Dr. Westmore resulted in a volunteer job offer. She realized that Isaac was studying her.

"Something is bothering you."

"Nay," she said. "I just wondered how hard it was for you to get off work."

He smiled. "It wasn't a problem." He studied her thoughtfully. "Why?"

It was now or never, she thought, but still she hesitated. "I just wondered."

"You want to make plans to go somewhere tomorrow? That might be difficult since I took today off from work."

She shrugged. She paused and then admitted, "I already have plans for tomorrow. I have appointment with the Westmore Clinic."

His expression filled with concern. "Are you ill?"

"*Nay*, I want to volunteer my time there." Unable to stop, Ellen went on to explain about the Yoders' daughter, and about the other couple she'd met and how she felt the need to do something to help. "I mentioned it to *Dat*, but he didn't want to hear it. He wants me to marry and have babies, and I will…someday. I thought if I could talk with Dr. Westmore, see if he would accept my help, then I could bring home enough information to convince *Dat* to give his permission."

Isaac had been silent as he listened to her talk. She studied his features carefully, wondering what he was thinking. Would he agree with her father? Or would he understand how important this was to her?

"When is your appointment?" he asked quietly.

She blushed. "Tomorrow at noon."

"*Nay.*"

She froze. "*Nay?* You don't think I should go?"

"I think you should go, but you should change your appointment so that I can come with you."

"I don't need you to come with me, but I appreciate the offer." Her heart filled with emotion. "I don't have far to go. I won't be going into the city. The clinic is on Old Philadelphia Pike."

He narrowed his gaze. "I still think you should change your appointment and let me come. I understand how important this is to you. Are you sure you'll be safe?"

"*Ja*, I'm certain." *He understands!* Ellen exhaled on a whoosh of relief. "I was afraid that you wouldn't understand."

"You thought I wouldn't approve like your *vadder*."

"I didn't know," she confessed softly. "I was afraid to tell you."

He didn't say anything for a minute. She shifted uncomfortably as he studied her.

"What are you looking at?" She touched her hair to see if something was out of place.

"You." He continued to study her as he took a sip from his soda, then set his cup down on the ground near his feet.

She cocked her head as her curiosity got the better of her. "Why?"

"You're different than you were."

Ellen frowned. "I'm still me."

"I'm glad of that, but it's something else." She didn't know how to respond. He stood and gazed down at her. "Will you tell me how things go with Dr. Westmore?" He looked as if he thought about insisting that he accompany her but then had thought better of it.

She nodded. "*Ja*, I may need to be consoled."

"I doubt it." He flashed a grin. They enjoyed the rest of their afternoon together. Isaac insisted on walking her home afterward. "Don't forget I'll be waiting to hear how things go tomorrow.

Ellen beamed at him. "I'll let you know. *Danki*, Isaac."

Chapter Fourteen

Ellen steered the horse-drawn buggy in the direction
of the Westmore Clinic. She was nervous. So much
hinged on her meeting with Dr. Westmore. If the doctor didn't use volunteers, as the employees in the office
had indicated, then there was every likelihood that he
would turn her away. But she had to try.

She stopped at a red light with the rest of traffic.
What would she do if this didn't work out? She didn't
know. She could only hope and pray that it would.

The clinic was a small brick building on Old Philadelphia Pike. Ellen recognized it immediately from her
last brief visit. She turned Blackie into the lot next to
the building and secured him to a hitching post. Hers
was the only buggy there. The knowledge gave her confidence, although she wouldn't have minded if she had
someone with her, like she did last time, when Mary
Ruth had come.

The young woman at the front desk stood up as she
took notice of Ellen when she walked in. "Can I help
you?"

"The appointment you made for me is for today," Ellen said as she sat down in the waiting room.

Joan's gaze widened. "Miss Mast?" She looked surprised as she studied her and Ellen suddenly realized that during her last visit she'd been dressed not in her own garments but as an *Englisher*.

"*Ja*, but it's Ellen," she corrected.

"I'll tell Dr. Westmore that you're here," Joan said, sounding a little friendlier than previously.

Joan was back within seconds. "His nurse isn't here. If you come with me, I'll take you to his office," she said.

Ellen rose from her chair on shaky legs. Now that the time had come for her meeting with Dr. Westmore, she was terrified. Everything hinged on today's encounter. This would be her last chance to convince her father to give her his permission to work here.

Ellen didn't know what she expected but it wasn't the nice-looking man in his midforties who greeted her as she was escorted in. Dr. Westmore rose from behind his desk. "You must be Ellen." He gestured toward the chair. "Have a seat. I have a half hour before my next patient. I heard that you'd like to be a volunteer here."

Ellen nodded. "I believe I can be of help with your patients' families. I know how difficult life is for couples of children with special needs. I understand them. I know about their faith, their way of life… I can show them understanding and help you get through to those who are having trouble making the right decision for the children they love who are sick." She blushed. She realized that she'd been rambling on without stopping. The doctor had remained silent while she'd talked. She couldn't tell if he was receptive to the idea or if he thought her presumptuous for making the suggestion.

"How did you know about us?" he asked.

She couldn't read his expression. "Rebekka and Caleb Yoder. Their daughter, Alice, is your patient. Alice has Crigler-Najjar syndrome—type 2. I know that the little girl struggles to live a normal life, that every single day she has to lie under a blue light to keep a toxic substance called bilirubin from poisoning her."

He eyed her thoughtfully. "You've certainly done your homework." He rubbed his chin. "Why do you want to help?"

"Because I feel like I can be of service. I picture myself in the Yoders' situation and I understand their pain. I know you are doing good work here, but you're not Amish." She blushed. "I don't mean to imply that you don't know how to medically treat your patients. But do you understand what it is to be raised Amish? To live by the *Ordnung*? To be conscious of the Lord's way?" She felt a rise in confidence. "I'm not saying that I am better than anyone. I'm not trained or certified like you or your staff, but I can help if you'll let me. I honestly want to help."

"I see." He picked up a pen and turned it over, end to end in a constant fluid motion that suggested he fingered the instrument that way frequently.

"Ellen, you've given me something to think about. How often do you think you could come in to work?"

"Two days a week?" Ellen knew it wasn't much time, but she still had chores to do at home. She couldn't abandon her way of life simply because she felt the need to volunteer there. She might be able to get her father to agree to one or two days.

"I like the idea," Dr. Westmore said. "But I have to check on a few things before I can decide whether or not to accept your kind offer. Is there a way I can reach you?"

Ellen gave him the number of Bob Whittier. "Bob will see that I get your message," she said. "I can call back if you leave a phone number and time."

He nodded, looking satisfied. He rose and Ellen realized that it was her cue to leave. "Thank you for coming in, Ellen."

"I appreciate your time," she replied. "Dr. Westmore, is there literature on some of the genetic conditions that are treated here in the clinic? I'd like some information to show my parents."

"Yes, of course." He frowned. "Are there genetic disorders in your family? Do you have a special-needs sibling?"

She shook her head. "*Nay*, not as far as I am aware. We are all fortunate to be healthy."

"Your friends Rebekka and Caleb—are they happy with my care?"

"*Ja*, that's why I'm here. They are grateful that you are concerned with their daughter's illness. They appreciate that you care about our sick Amish children."

"I do what I can." He came out from behind the desk to escort her to the front reception area. "I'll be in touch," he said as they stepped into the front room.

"Thank you, Dr. Westmore."

He nodded, then turned with a smile to greet a young Amish couple who must have come in while they were in his office. They had waited patiently with their young child. Ellen saw that the little boy had a medical condition, but she didn't know what. She turned to leave.

"Ellen," Joan, the receptionist, said as Ellen started toward the door. "Dr. Westmore asked me to give you these." She handed Ellen numerous pamphlets. It was the information she'd requested.

"Thank you." She left, feeling optimistic after what had transpired during her meeting with Dr. Westmore. She suddenly had a good feeling about the job offer she wanted and about her future…until she exited the building and discovered Isaac Lapp waiting for her in the parking lot. He was leaning against her vehicle, his expression unreadable as he watched her approach.

Chapter Fifteen

"What are you doing here, Isaac?"

Isaac narrowed his gaze as he studied her. "I'm waiting for you."

"Why?"

"Because I wanted to know how you made out." He eyed her with amusement. "Did you think I followed you to make sure you were all right?"

She nodded. "You wanted to keep an eye on me, but I got here fine. If you're worried about Brad, he won't be coming back. You scared him off."

Did she really think that? "I'm afraid you're mistaken if you think he's given up being a nuisance. It's not like him to give up."

She looked suddenly uncomfortable. "I haven't seen him today. I'm not heading into the city. This is as far as I'm going. I doubt I'll encounter him on the way home."

He studied her, noting her flushed cheeks. "I didn't follow you, Ellen." He glanced across the street to the construction site where he was currently working. "I didn't follow you."

"You didn't?"

"*Nay*, I didn't have to. Once you mentioned the address, I knew exactly where you were going. So I came over."

She narrowed her gaze. "Why?"

"For you." Isaac folded his arms across his chest. "I've decided to make everything *you* do my business."

She bristled. "What are trying to do, Isaac? Upset me?"

He laughed. "I'm sorry. I'm teasing you and I shouldn't. Especially when I want us to be *gut* friends again."

She didn't understand. "Then why are you here?" She eyed him warily. "And don't say again that you wanted to know how I made out? Where did you come from?"

He grinned as he gestured toward a house under construction in the lot across the street. "I'm working over there. I had just taken my lunch break when I saw you pull in."

"That's Matt Rhoades's current project," she muttered, appearing to relax.

"Ja." He examined her closely. His gaze focused on the house across the street again before he returned his attention to Ellen. "So, how did you make out with Dr. Westmore?" From the moment she'd pulled her buggy into the lot, he'd wanted to accompany her inside to lend his support. "It went *oll recht*, I suppose"

She looked less than pleased. "He didn't offer me the position yet, but he did give me some information to give to my *mudder* and *vadder*."

"What did he say?" He sent her a look that silently begged her to confide in him.

Her expression changed as if she'd come to a decision. "That he'd think about it and get back with me."

"'Tis something, isn't it?" He glanced at the building. "I never paid attention to this place before." And now he was curious because of Ellen's interest and because of what she'd told him about the children who were helped here.

"*Ja*, 'tis something, but I was hoping for more."

"It will work out, Ellen. You just have to have faith."

"Like you have faith?" she quipped then her face turned bright red with embarrassment. "I'm sorry. That was uncalled for." To his surprise, she reached out to touch his arm. "I am sorry, Isaac. I know things have been difficult for you since…"

Her words hurt but there was truth behind what she'd implied. "I'm fine, Ellen. And, *ja*, I do have faith. That hasn't changed." It didn't mean that he felt deserving of church membership.

She looked contrite. "I'm hurt because you won't talk to me about what happened."

He felt a sudden chill. "I'm not ready to talk about it. With anyone." He glanced toward the job site to see if any of the other workers had returned from lunch. He wasn't ready for this discussion. "I hope you get your offer soon," he said softly. He couldn't be mad at her. She only wanted to know the truth and he was afraid to talk about that night at Whittier's Store. He should get back but still he lingered. "Tell me more about what is wrong with the Yoders' child. You told me she was sick with some sort of genetic disease."

"Alice has Crigler-Najjar syndrome—type 2. It's a disease where a toxic substance called bilirubin builds up in her blood, turning her yellow. Her disorder forces her to lie under a special blue light for ten to twelve hours every day."

Isaac felt compassion for the young couple. "That must be terrible for the child and her parents." He lifted himself away from her buggy. "You feel bad for them. No wonder you want to get involved." He ran fingers through his hair. "You, Ellen, have a warm and generous spirit," he said approvingly. "I think it's a wise thing you're doing. I'm sure the Lord will approve."

She blushed, apparently embarrassed by the compliment, and looked away briefly.

She sighed. "I'm glad you understand, Isaac. My *dat* doesn't. If these brochures don't help, then I have no hope of working here." She met his gaze with blue eyes filled with an emotion bordering on pleasure. "*Danki* for coming to find out how the appointment went."

"Of course I want to know. You are a *gut* person, Ellen. You care about people." His lips twisted in self-derision. "Even those who refuse to see how much you care when they should." He was referring to himself and the way she'd tried to warn him about Nancy but he'd refused to listen. He saw that she watched him closely. He gestured to the literature she held. He raised his eyebrows. "May I see the information you have to convince your *dat*?"

"*Ja.*" She handed a brochure to him. "I just hope it makes a difference."

He looked over the information and smiled. "I believe it will. I'll pray that it does."

"*Danki*, Isaac." She seemed pleased. Her expression softened as she continued to study him. "Is there anything else you'd like to talk about?"

"Can we get together again soon? Maybe go for lunch instead of ice cream? I do have something I need to tell you, but I'd rather not discuss it here." He handed the brochure back to her.

She hesitated. "I guess we could." But she appeared reluctant.

"Just a meal, Ellen."

"*Oll recht.* When?"

"Tomorrow?" He didn't want to wait any longer. He'd already waited too long as it was.

Why hadn't he understood sooner? *Because I was too taken by Nancy to think about what I'd done to Ellen.*

After Nancy had left, he had struggled to get over the breakup and the realization that Nancy wasn't the person he'd thought she was. He should have gone to Ellen immediately, apologized and told her that she was right, but it had been months since he'd spent any time with her. And he'd been unwilling to admit that he'd done a terrible thing to Ellen by refusing to trust in what she had to say.

He waited for Ellen's answer to his request. She was quiet, reflective. "What time?"

"Eleven thirty?"

She nodded. "I will meet you at eleven thirty. Where?"

"I'll come for you." Like he used to, he thought but didn't want to say it.

"*Oll recht.*" She avoided his glance, seemed suddenly eager to leave. "I have to go."

"I'll see you tomorrow, Ellen." He watched as she threw the brochures she'd received from the doctor onto the other side of the front seat, then climbed into the buggy and picked up the leathers. He saw her give him a concerned look. "Don't worry about our discussion, Ellen. 'Tis nothing bad." At least, not for her, he hoped. But it would be difficult for him admitting that he'd been wrong, for he was afraid that by resurrecting the past, he would effectively be sending her away. He didn't know what he'd do if she wouldn't forgive him. He didn't know what he'd do if she avoided him in the future and forced him from her life.

The next morning Ellen waited for Isaac near the road on her father's farm property. She couldn't help wondering what he wanted to discuss. He'd told her she shouldn't be concerned, that it was nothing bad, but that didn't keep her from worrying.

It was a warm day. She'd finished all of her chores early. She'd told her mother that she was going out for a while. *Mam* had been too busy to ask any questions. Miriam Zook was coming to visit, and her mother was waiting for her to arrive. Fortunately, *Mam* didn't ask her to stay. She wasn't sure what she'd have told her if she had. She didn't want to bring Isaac's name into any conversation with her parents. Ever since Isaac had gotten in trouble two years ago, her mother and father had acted as if they were disappointed in him, that it bothered them that he'd never given any details of what happened.

Isaac appeared, and she watched his approach. He raised his hand in greeting, and heart thumping hard, she waved back.

He smiled as he drew closer, and her lips curved in response.

"*Hallo*, Ellen Mast," he said warmly.

She melted inside. "*Hallo*. Where are we going for lunch?"

"What would you like for lunch? A burger?" He fell in step with her as they started down the street.

"Are you buying?" It seemed for a moment that time had reversed itself and they were close friends who bantered about who would pay for their meal and what kind of soda they would order and which one tasted better. They had different opinions on soda flavors. She had liked root beer, while Isaac had liked cream soda. At one time, they'd teased each other often in this way. "*Ja*, I'm buying," he said with a twinkle in his gray eyes.

"Then I'll have soup and a sandwich."

"No burger?" He feigned momentary disappointment. Then he grinned. "Soup and sandwich it is."

They walked without speaking. Surprisingly to Ellen, the silence between them was relaxed, friendly, without the tension that had been between them when they'd chosen stargazing over their community youth singing. But their time together hadn't been long. Things had gone downhill quickly and she wasn't even sure why that night had turned sour for them.

Whittier's Store loomed ahead. They had to pass it as they walked the remaining distance to the restaurant in silence. Ellen's thoughts turned to the night that the store had been vandalized. She'd never believed that Isaac was guilty, although others had believed that he was. He wouldn't have done anything to hurt Bob Whittier, a neighbor and friend to their community. She and Isaac had enjoyed too many ice-cream cones and sodas here for her to believe that Isaac would suddenly turn on a man who was always kind to them. Ever since it had happened, she'd been bothered by the fact that her former friend had taken the blame. Even when she'd been angry and hurt because of him, she'd still thought Isaac incapable of the crime.

They reached the restaurant. The bells clanged as Isaac opened the entrance door and gestured for Ellen to precede him.

At the sound, the hostess looked up from where she stood behind the podium. "Two today?"

Isaac nodded. Ellen felt heat rise to her cheeks as the hostess studied them a moment before going to see if there was a table available for them.

"Maybe they carry mint chocolate chip ice cream at their ice cream counter next door," Isaac said.

The hostess returned in time to hear Isaac's comment. Her eyes lit up with pleasure. "We most certainly have mint chocolate chip ice cream."

"Maybe we'll have some dessert," Isaac said, smiling at Ellen.

Ellen grinned, feeling suddenly happy. They followed the young hostess to a booth next to a window.

"Is this all right?" the young woman asked.

"It's fine. Thank you," Ellen assured her.

Ellen enjoyed a bowl of split pea with ham soup and a turkey sandwich. Isaac ordered and enjoyed his hamburger and fries. When they were done, Isaac paid the check and they rose to leave. The ice cream was sold in a glass case in the store connected to the restaurant. Ellen leaned against the glass case, eyeing the large containers of colorful ice cream that invited one to taste.

"Two mint chocolate chip ice-cream cones," Isaac ordered. "One single scoop for me and one double for my friend Ellen here."

Ellen laughed. "*Nay*, make that two single-scoop cones," she said, flashing Isaac a teasing glance.

His expression warmed as she corrected his order. "Are you sure you don't want a double?"

She shook her head. "*Nay*, but that doesn't mean you can't have one."

He appeared to be fighting a smile. "Since I'm paying, a single scoop will be plenty."

She wrinkled up her nose at him. "You can afford a double for both of us, Isaac Lapp, and you know it." They took their ice cream cones and went outside to enjoy them in the warm sunshine. The restaurant had dining tables on a deck in the front of the building. They gravitated to a table and sat down. As he ate, Isaac smiled at her.

"Just like old times," Ellen commented.

A flicker in his expression suggested that he liked that she'd remembered.

Isaac smiled at her. "How's your ice cream?" He took a lick of his cone."

"*Gut*. Yours?"

"The same. *Gut* as usual."

The day felt good. The air between her and Isaac was relaxed. Suddenly Ellen remembered why she'd agreed to meet him today. Isaac had something he'd wanted to discuss with her.

"Isaac…"

"Ellen…"

They had spoken at the same time. They laughed but a sudden tension had cropped up between them, as if they'd both recalled that going for ice cream together was no longer a normal occurrence for them.

"Go ahead, Isaac," she invited.

"About what happened…to our friendship," he began. "I'm sorry. We were friends and I didn't listen to you.

You tried to tell me what Nancy was like, and I…" He exhaled sharply and looked away a moment. His gray eyes held regret when he turned to face her again. "I didn't listen. As I recall, I wasn't…kind."

Ellen felt her throat tighten as it all came back to her. The last thing she'd expected was an apology from him. It had been a long time, after all. "Why now?" she asked.

He looked sheepish. "I miss you."

She shook her head. "Isaac—"

"I'm sorry, Ellen. I know it won't change anything between us, but I needed you to know that I was wrong and I'm sincerely sorry for what I said…for the way I hurt you."

"You did hurt me," she whispered. Feeling the sudden need to put distance between them as she processed his apology, Ellen stood and walked a few feet away. She didn't look at him. She was afraid if she did, then she'd do or say something she'd regret. She had longed for his apology. It had finally come, but while she appreciated that it had come at all, the words seemed to have arrived too late to make much of a difference.

She turned, stared without seeing. The street came into focus. Several cars passed by. One turned and pulled into the lot, perhaps tempted by the image of an ice cream cone on a sign on the front lawn. Years ago, she and Isaac came here on occasion. The restaurant called the Hungry Hog was enjoyed by locals and tourists alike. Isaac hadn't said a word after he'd apologized. Ellen wondered if she could trust that things would get better, but she had doubts, considering that her feelings for him were stronger than his for her, just as it had been years ago. She could accept his apology, but could things go back to the way they were? She thought not. She wouldn't be hurt by him again.

She wondered how much she really knew about Isaac. She had thought she'd understood him once, but now she wondered. She turned to face him. "What happened at Whittier's Store that night, Isaac? I find it hard to believe that you spray-painted Bob's siding." She kept going, although she saw how he'd closed off his expression. "I don't believe you had anything to do with vandalizing his place, although I believe you made restitution, because that's the way you are. I think someone else did the nasty deed. I don't know why you took the blame or why you paid for the repairs, but I can't see you doing something like that." She shifted on her seat. She had always wondered what had happened, but she couldn't have asked him, because they were no longer friends by that point.

"Tell me what happened, Isaac." She touched his arm. "Tell me. You know you can confide in me."

"Ellen…" This time her name was an agonized whisper. "I'm sorry but I can't talk about it."

"Can't or won't?" She had thought that if he'd open up to her, then she'd know that he was willing to trust her. The fact that he was reluctant told her that despite his apology, nothing between them had really changed.

"I can't." He swallowed hard. "I'm sorry."

She shuddered out a sigh. "I won't ask again, but I will say this—there is no way you did it. You're innocent and I have always believed that and always will. But it hurts me that you still don't trust me enough to tell me."

"Ellen, I care for you, I do, but you want me to tell you about something that doesn't only concern me."

She blinked. "You're protecting someone." She bit her lip. "Nancy?"

"Nay!"

He'd been so quick to defend Nancy that she wondered if he still wasn't over her. Pain radiated through to her heart. She loved him, but she had to keep her distance.

"I am sorry."

She shrugged as if unconcerned. "I should go…" She managed to smile. "*Danki* for the meal and the cone."

"Ellen."

"I can get home by myself. I'll be fine, I promise." She spied Nate Peachy as he drove a pony cart. It had been a while since she'd talked with her friend. "Nate!" she cried. He pulled up on the leathers and stopped the vehicle. She hurried across the road to meet him, ignoring Isaac when he called out to her to come back. She was blinded by tears as she reached Nate. The young man took one look at her and then at Isaac. He grabbed her arm.

"Come with me," Nate said. "I'll take you home." He turned back the way he'd come, pulling her to follow. "Are you *oll recht*?"

She sniffed. "I… I will be."

He flashed Isaac an angry glance. She hadn't told Nate what was wrong; he had figured it out on his own. She suspected that he knew, had always known, how she felt about Isaac. Nate was the kind of friend she felt comfortable with. She could rely on Nate. He'd been there for her when Isaac hadn't been.

Chapter Sixteen

It was visiting Sunday, and Mae and Amos King were hosting. Isaac got up early that morning to do his chores. Since it was the Lord's day, the only thing he needed to do was feed the animals, and for that he was grateful. Since Ellen had left with Nate, he hadn't slept much. His days and nights were filled with her image: the way she looked as she enjoyed her ice cream, her smile when she was amused, the warmth in her blue eyes when she was pleased with something, the intensity of her expression when she'd told him that she believed in him, in his innocence.

He hadn't seen Ellen since the day he'd taken her to lunch. The loss was slowly killing him inside.

As he'd watched Ellen leave with Nate that day, Isaac had realized that it was over. He had lost his chance at making things right. He had apologized but it hadn't made a difference. She wanted something he couldn't give her—the truth.

He swallowed against a painful lump as he recalled how easily Ellen had gone off with Nate. He'd felt jealousy raise its ugly head. He'd wanted to run after her, tell her that he loved her…confess the truth about what happened that night at Whittier's, but he couldn't. It was Henry Yoder's secret, and until his friend came forward with the truth, he had to continue to live with the lie, although it bothered him to do it. This lie was a sin he couldn't confess and he wondered whether or not things would ever change.

He loved Ellen, more than he'd ever loved anyone. He should have been rejoicing at the realization, except he couldn't. He wasn't good for her. He'd made mistakes that couldn't be fixed. He'd hurt her once, and then he'd hurt her again. He was unworthy of her love.

As he fed and watered the horses, Isaac realized that it would be best if he continued to keep his distance from her. She deserved better than him. He wanted her to be happy, even if it was with another man. *Like Nate.*

Isaac closed his eyes and groaned.

Ellen was in high spirits as she dressed for visiting Sunday at the Amos Kings. On Friday, Bob Whittier had brought her a message from the Westmore Clinic. Dr. Westmore wanted to offer her a job—not as a volunteer as she'd requested but as a paid part-time employee. She'd suffered mixed feelings at first. She wanted to accept the position but she had yet to convince her father. As soon as Bob had left, Ellen had sought out her father where he worked in the barn.

"Dat," she called as she entered the dark interior of the structure.

"In here, Ellen," he replied.

She located him by his voice. He was in the back stables, looking over the pair of goats they kept here.

"I need to talk with you."

He rose from a crouch. "What's wrong?"

"Nothing…" She closed her eyes. "*Dat*, I've been offered a paid part-time job." She bit her lip. "At the Westmore children's clinic." She stood, fearing his rebuke. When she had returned from her appointment, she'd placed the brochures from the clinic where her parents could find them. *Dat* had never mentioned seeing them, and she'd never spoken of her visit.

"I see." He eyed her with displeasure.

"Please, *Dat*. I really want to do this—need to do this," she said. "I would have worked there for nothing, but now I've been asked to work and get paid."

He didn't say anything at first, and waiting for his reply, Ellen felt a burning in her stomach. "*Dat*, I didn't take the job. I wouldn't accept it without your permission."

He remained silent, his expression thoughtful. "Why do you want to do this so badly?"

"I feel that the Lord has asked me to do this." She spoke passionately and from the heart. "The clinic is working on ways to help children, *Dat*. Children from the Amish community. I know I can help. I know parents will talk to me. I can help by listening to them and helping the doctor with treatment and care—and with understanding our beliefs."

Her father didn't say a word until she gave him the literature from the clinic. She showed him information about the different types of genetic conditions that the children of Amish parents were sometimes born with. She told him about some of the treatments the children had to endure just to stay alive. And her father asked questions, which she answered as best she could.

"We are fortunate, *Dat*. The Lord blessed us all with

good health. Please give me your permission to work there. It's only for two days a week."

Her father blinked several times as if he was deeply affected by what he'd learned. *Dat* was quiet for a moment. *"Ja,"* he whispered. "You may work there."

She thanked him with tears in her eyes. *"Danki, Dat."*

He managed to smile for her.

"Mam..." Ellen began.

"She'll give her blessing. We talked about it when you first mentioned it. I didn't like it, but your *mudder* had a different opinion." He smiled. "You'd better go and call Dr. Westmore back. Tell him that you'll be happy to accept his offer."

And so she'd called him back. She was to start on this coming Tuesday. Ellen felt lighthearted as well as excited about her new job...as long as she focused on her good fortune rather than her feelings for Isaac.

She would be working with special children and helping their families! Her good humor stayed with her as they rode in their family buggy to the Amos Kings. It didn't dampen immediately when she saw Isaac arrive with his family. Ellen felt her joy dissipate when Isaac glanced at her coldly, then promptly looked away.

It was only after the arrival of the Abram Peachy family that Ellen made an effort to recapture the pleasure of the day, for Nate Peachy, the deacon's son, was happy to see her. In fact, he immediately headed in her direction after spying her in the yard.

"Ellen," he said with a warm smile.

She grinned at him. "Nate."

"'Tis *gut* to see you."

"And you," she said.

"How are you doing?" Nate studied her with male appreciation, which was a balm to her wounded ego.

"I'm…managing." She brightened. "I got a job at the Westmore Clinic." She had told him about it when he'd taken her home after she and Isaac had argued.

"Want to take a walk with me later? You can tell me all about it then."

She nodded. "That would be nice."

"When?" He seemed eager to go, and she felt pleasure in the knowledge.

"After lunch? Or we could sit and enjoy the sun," she suggested.

He appeared pleased by her suggestion. "*Ja*, we could."

Nate found a spot in the warm sun where they could sit on the lawn and enjoy conversation. Ellen felt someone's regard and saw Isaac's eyes on her. When she looked at him, he quickly glanced away. She saw him talking with his younger brothers and a friend. She saw him say something to Daniel, heard him laugh at his brother's reply…and Ellen tried not to feel hurt that he had accepted the end of their friendship so easily.

Instead she concentrated on Nate, who was clearly more interested in her than Isaac Lapp was. They ate the midday meal and then went for a walk afterward. They crossed the street to the swing set in the schoolyard. Ellen settled on a swing and Nate took the one next to her. He kept up a commentary on the proper way to pump one's feet in order to swing higher.

"Try it, Ellen," he said. "Watch me first!"

Ellen watched with amusement as Nate pumped his feet back and forth to make his swing soar. She laughed as she tried it without luck until she watched Nate again.

She was able to duplicate the movement of his feet. She felt the air rush against her skin, the laughter rise in her throat as she swung to and fro in glorious abandonment.

"Fun, *ja?*" Nate asked.

She grinned at him, "*Ja. Danki* for bringing me here."

"My pleasure," he said, sounding as if he meant it.

She felt joy that she could enjoy the simple happiness of riding on a swing. Then suddenly she experienced a strange frisson of sensation at her nape, traveling down to her heels. She looked up and saw Isaac Lapp standing across the road, watching her...watching her with Nate. And she knew a longing for what she couldn't have. *Isaac Lapp's love.* She looked away, determined to enjoy herself with Nate. But her feelings for Isaac remained heavily in her mind.

Ellen woke up the next day after a night's fitful sleep. She still couldn't get Isaac out of her mind. She should have gone over to say *hallo. When he glanced at you and you looked back, he turned away.*

Did it bother Isaac to see her with Nate? She wasn't trying to make him jealous. She'd needed someone to talk to, to care.

She had promised her mother she would go shopping for her today. There were several things she needed, but *Mam* claimed that she was too busy to go.

She felt groggy, disoriented. She went into the bathroom and splashed cold water on her face. It helped to wake her but she thought that she'd feel even better after a strong cup of coffee with breakfast. She dressed quickly and went downstairs. She found her mother in the kitchen, working on her shopping list.

"Sleep well?" she asked as she grabbed a mug from the cabinet and poured herself coffee from the pot on the stove. To her relief, the brew was still hot.

Mam studied her as Ellen sat down at the kitchen table across from her. "I slept well enough." Her eyes narrowed. "You didn't."

"I couldn't sleep."

"It's because of that young man."

Ellen's heart skipped a beat. "Who?"

"Nate Peachy. I saw the two of you yesterday. You had fun with him."

She managed to smile. "*Ja*, I did." She couldn't tell her mother who'd actually been on her mind all night and into the early hours of the morning. It was Isaac, not Nate, who was constantly in her thoughts.

"I've invited the Peachys over for supper this evening."

Ellen felt a jolt. "You did?"

Mam nodded. "Thought you'd enjoy it."

"I—" She looked down. "I would." Nate Peachy was easy to spend time with and she had enjoyed herself with him, but she didn't feel for him as she did for Isaac. She didn't believe she ever would.

"Is something wrong?" *Mam* asked, furrowing her brow.

"*Nay*." Ellen gave her a genuine smile. She would enjoy having the Peachys over. She just hoped that Nate didn't expect more from her than she could give him.

"*Gut!*" *Mam* scribbled down a few more items. "Here you go," she said as she handed her the list.

Ellen looked over its contents. "What is all this for?" She'd read chili powder, a can of mild green chilies, a bag of flour and several other unusual items.

"I thought I'd try a new recipe for our dinner guests tonight."

She looked at her mother with skepticism. "*Mam*, I don't want to change your plans, but do you think that's wise? What if they don't like chili powder and green chilies?"

Mam gave it some thought. "You're right. Give me the list."

Stifling a small smile, Ellen handed it back to her. She watched with satisfaction as her mother scratched off the first two items and added a few more at the bottom.

When she received it back, Ellen perused the list and nodded with satisfaction. "You're going to make chicken and drop dumplings." She was pleased. "They are going to love them. It's your specialty."

Mam beamed at her. "You should be able to get everything I need at Yoder's."

Ellen nodded. She quickly ate a bowl of cereal and finished her coffee. By the time she'd finished, she felt a whole lot better and more awake.

"I'll head over there now," Ellen said as she stood and brought her bowl and cup to the sink, where she washed them. She suddenly realized how quiet it was. "Where are *Dat* and the boys?"

"Your *vadder* went over to Horseshoe Joe's, something about discussing some new crops. Your *bruders* went with him. They wanted to see Peter. They're fond of him. Peter is kind to them."

Ellen agreed. Peter Zook was a kind man who always treated everyone fairly. He lived the life laid out by the *Ordnung* even though he hadn't joined the church yet.

Why couldn't she fall for someone like Peter? Not

that she would have a chance, she realized, since Peter was in love with Meg Stoltzfus and had been for a long time. *Peter is like me, loving someone who doesn't feel the same way.*

And she didn't believe that Meg regarded him as a friend. She reacted to Peter as if she thought him more of a nuisance than anything.

The ride to Yoder's General Store was pleasant, although clouds had started to gather in the sky and it looked like it might rain at any moment. Sure enough, by time she parked the buggy and tied up Blackie next to the building, it had begun to drizzle.

Ellen ran into the store, glad to make it inside before the rain fell in earnest. "*Gut* morning, Margaret," she greeted before she turned and saw that it wasn't Margaret behind the counter but her son. "Henry! *Hallo!*"

"*Hallo*, Ellen," Henry said, glancing away as he did so. He didn't seem happy that he had to work in the store this morning.

"How have you been? I haven't seen you in a long time."

"*Ja*, I've been busy." He met her gaze, but there was something off in his expression that bothered her. "Building furniture and things, over in Ephrata."

"So your *mudder* said." She eyed the young man carefully, noting certain changes in him. He had aged since she'd last seen him. He didn't look well, as if he wasn't particularly happy with his life. "I used to see you at singings and sometimes with Isaac."

Henry jerked at the mention of Isaac. Ellen narrowed her gaze. "Your parents have forbidden you to spend time with Isaac, haven't they?" she guessed. "Because of what he did that night at Whittier's Store."

Henry looked uncomfortable, even guilty, as he fiddled with something beneath the counter.

"Henry?"

He shrugged. "I…" He seemed to stand straighter. "Can I help you find something?" he asked, changing the subject.

"I guess I should get shopping, *ja*?" She held up her list. "*Mam* is waiting for these items to fix supper for friends tonight."

He relaxed and seemed relieved. "Let me know if you have trouble finding anything."

As she walked about the store, finding the items she needed to purchase, Ellen pondered the reason for Henry's odd behavior. Now that she gave it some thought, Henry's absence since the store vandalism incident seemed strange. He and Isaac had been friends who had gone on *rumspringa* together. And he avoided his friend? He hadn't agreed that his parents had put a stop to his and Isaac's friendship…which had to mean that there was another reason that Henry stayed away.

Ellen frowned as she grabbed the last item on her mother's shopping list. Henry had looked almost guilty when she'd mentioned Isaac. Ellen knew that Isaac was innocent of the crime. She'd always felt it, known it to be true.

But what about Henry? Was Henry there that night? He used to hang out with Brad Smith and the others. Henry had liked Jessica, if Ellen remembered correctly, who'd been Nancy's friend. Had Henry painted graffiti on the back exterior wall of Bob Whittier's store?

Clutching the items her mother needed, Ellen returned to the front to pay. She set everything on the counter and watched as Henry began to add the price of her items on a paper bag.

He looked up from his math. "That makes a total of $20.42."

Ellen dug the money out of her change purse and silently gave it to him.

He nodded and then put the money into the old cash register and gave her change. Then he turned the bag around so that she could check his math.

"I trust you," she said, turning the bag back around without checking.

He blushed guiltily as if her words had upset him.

"Henry," she said. "You don't seem yourself. What's going on?"

"What do you mean?" he shot back defensively. "Nothing's going on. Why would you ask?" He looked nervous, and Ellen was suspicious. She knew he was lying; she could tell that something was wrong.

She studied him, trying to get a read. She'd speak her mind and suffer the consequences. "You were there the night Bob Whittier's place was spray-painted, weren't you?" She drew in a deep breath before plunging on. "Did you do it, Henry? Is that why you don't come around anymore? Is that why you've been avoiding Isaac since it happened? Isaac took the blame for you, didn't he? And you're ashamed."

Henry turned pale. "I…" He shook his head as if he wanted to deny the truth but couldn't. *"Ja,"* he whispered. "I was there at the store that night." He hesitated. "I was involved."

Ellen felt sympathy as she looked at him. Henry was clearly suffering as much as Isaac, if not more. Except that Henry was guilty and Isaac was innocent. "You need to come forward and tell the truth."

"Nay!" he gasped. "I can't!" He was shaking his head. "I won't."

"I won't tell anyone, Henry. It's not for me to say. Isaac took the blame for you and he's never said a word. I knew he was innocent, but he wouldn't admit to anything." She eyed him with disappointment coupled with compassion. "The confession must come from you when you're ready." She picked up one grocery bag. Henry had yet to bag the rest of her items. "It's hurting you not to tell. If you confess and tell the elders that you're sorry, then you'll be forgiven. People won't care that you were afraid to speak up. As long as you're sorry and say so."

"I can't," he said, looking sick. "He said he'd kill me if I did."

"Kill you!" she gasped. "Who?"

"Brad Smith."

Ellen shuddered, recalling the two times Brad had tried to intimidate her. "He's not a *gut* person."

Henry bobbed his head. "I would have told the truth, but I was scared."

"But if you did tell the truth, Brad would be arrested and put in jail…"

"Then my parents would hate me," he said, "and so would everyone else."

"And how do you think Isaac feels? He's been regarded as a criminal because he stood up for you, and he never told a soul."

"He must have told you."

"Nay. He didn't. I guessed. You were acting so strange." She shifted the bag, which had grown heavy

as she held it. "Now I know why he wouldn't tell me." And she felt lighter for knowing the truth, for knowing that Isaac's heart was in the right place. "He's been protecting you."

Henry didn't respond. She watched as he put the remainder of her items in a bag with shaking hands. "Henry, think about it. *Ja?*"

He nodded but looked miserable. She feared that he didn't possess the strength to come forward with the truth.

She grabbed the last bag. "It was nice to see you again, Henry," she said politely.

And then she left. Her thoughts were filled with Henry and Isaac and their situation. Isaac had lied to protect his friend, because he had a good heart. But he wouldn't see it that way. He would focus on the actual lie itself, a lie that weighed heavily on his mind because he couldn't confess his sin to the church deacon without getting his friend into serious trouble. And so Isaac struggled with indecision—and felt less of a man because of it. If Henry came forward, Isaac would feel better because everyone would know the truth and he could ask for and be given forgiveness. But he would never confess... The truth would have to come from Henry.

Tears filled Ellen's eyes as she got into her buggy and drove home. She realized that she loved Isaac even more than ever, if it was possible. She wondered if she'd ever get over her love for him.

Nate was coming to supper with the rest of his family. She would talk with him and make him understand that they could be only friends. She'd feared that their relationship had changed. Their friendship had been comfortable. Nate had known about her feelings for

Isaac without her telling him, and he'd understood what she'd needed. She didn't want their friendship to change. Nate could never be Isaac.

Tomorrow she would start work at the clinic. It was something to focus on, something good, a worthy task to take her mind off the situation while she offered her attention and help to those who needed it.

But she'd be thinking of Isaac because she thought about him constantly and she knew that wouldn't change.

Chapter Seventeen

Dinner with the Abram Peachys was a boisterous affair with loud conversation and good humor. After enjoying her mother's drop dumplings and chicken along with peas, chowchow, macaroni salad and dried-corn casserole, Ellen found herself walking about the property with Nate Peachy. For some reason, she couldn't bring herself to head toward her grandfather's bench, where she and Isaac had spent times together, talking and enjoying each other's company. It would seem like a betrayal if she brought Nate there to her and Isaac's special place. So she guided him in another direction, toward the right and outside the pasture fence.

The weather had cleared, and the landscape seemed awash with vibrant color. The pasture itself was a bright green. The scents of flowers and the aroma of horse filled the air, and Ellen loved it.

"'Twas nice of your *mudder* to invite us," Nate said.

She turned to him with her lips curved. "She's like that." She hesitated. "Your *dat* seems happy with Charlotte."

He nodded. "He is. Charlotte is *gut* for him. She's a *gut mudder* to all of us." He grew quiet. "*Dat* loves her."

Ellen was silent a long moment as she struggled over what to say. "Nate—"

"We're friends, Ellen," he said as if he'd anticipated what she wanted to say. "Nothing more. I know you have strong feelings for Isaac."

"I don't know how you knew, but you did." She regarded him with warmth. "What you did for me after Isaac…" She inhaled sharply. "Stepping in to be my friend when I was hurting and needed one. Taking me home. I'll never forget what you did for me, Nate."

He nodded, looking amused. "Nate Peachy at your service," he teased.

"I'm sorry," she mumbled. "I've made you uncomfortable."

"*Nay*, you haven't. We're friends. We enjoy each other's company. Someday I may need a friend." His gaze darkened. "There is someone…although she doesn't know and she's not ready."

Ellen studied his face, saw him blush. "Who?"

"Charlie."

"Stoltzfus?" she asked. He nodded. "She is young. Does she share your feelings?"

"*Nay*, I doubt she even knows who I am."

"Nate, if you like her, why spend time with me? She'll never know who you are if you're not making her aware of you. You need to talk with her every chance you can get. This Sunday after service."

"She's a child."

"Children grow up quickly," she said. Ellen shook her head. "Here I am giving advice when I've made a mess of things for myself."

"You're trying to help," he said. "And I'll give it some thought. You haven't made a mess of things—not with Isaac." He stared at her, and she squirmed uncomfortably. She felt as if he could see into her soul. "Isaac cares for you, but he won't admit it, because he doesn't feel as if he's right for you."

"I should be the one to decide that."

"I agree."

"Isaac feels the need to protect me. He sees me as a friend," she said with a sigh. "I don't want to be just a friend to him."

Nate grabbed hold of her *kapp* string and tugged playfully, like an older brother would do to his younger sister. "You need to let him know how you feel."

"I want to, but I don't want to get hurt again."

"Love is worth the risk of heartache, Ellen. Say you will talk with him."

"I will talk with him."

"Say it again with more confidence."

"I will to talk with him," she said with resolve.

"Perfect." He gave her a warm smile. "We should head back. We don't want our families thinking something that isn't so."

They started to head back when Ellen stopped. "Nate?"

"Ja?"

"Danki."

He nodded with brotherly affection. "I should be thanking you."

She shook her head. "I wish you success…with Charlie."

"I won't wish you success, Ellen. I know that you've already won."

They headed back to join their families. The Peachys

left shortly afterward, and Ellen went to bed with much to think about—Isaac, her first day of work at the Westmore Clinic for Special Children…but mostly about Isaac.

She had to make him see himself as she did…as a wonderful man who had stood up for a friend, a man worthy of God and a man who had already won her love.

Isaac felt terrible. He'd lost sleep over the last few nights. Seeing Ellen with Nate Peachy, despite wanting what was best for Ellen, had hurt him. But what else could he do? She deserved the best—and it wasn't him.

He'd arrived home from work about an hour ago. Since he and Daniel were late leaving the job site, *Mam* had supper on the table by the time the two of them had washed up outside and walked in.

Talk was lively around the table, as it usually was in the Lapp household. Isaac worked hard to be included. He didn't want anyone to guess that anything was wrong. He must have been successful, because no one in his family suspected that he was unhappy.

When the meal was over, Isaac escaped the house using the legitimate excuse of caring for the farm animals. The days were getting longer and he was glad that the sun was still out as he walked over to the barn. It was dark in the interior of the structure, however, so it took a minute for his eyes to adjust enough that he could see.

He went to check on the horses first. Someone stepped out from a stall, blocking his way, startling him.

"Isaac." Ellen stood close. He could smell the scent of her homemade lavender soap mingled with her store-bought shampoo.

His heart continued to hammer hard and his palms grew damp as he recognized her. Joy filled his heart but he quickly tamped it down. He didn't know why Ellen Lapp was in his barn, but he was more than ready to find out.

"What are you doing here, Ellen?" He hated that his tone was brisk, disapproving. He wanted her to be here, but he was afraid to hope…to want…to love.

His brusqueness must have struck her silent, for she'd backed away without a word. *It's for her own good*, he thought.

"I need to talk with you," she said. Her voice trembled, alerting him to the fact that he'd just hurt her, that she had something she wanted to say but was afraid.

He closed his eyes, scolding himself for being all kinds of foolish. "About what?" He gentled his tone. "What do you need to talk about?" He saw relief settle gently on her features. He looked down and realized that she was twisting her hands together anxiously. He edged closer until he could feel the heat from her body, the warmth of her skin. "First tell me why you thought the barn would be a *gut* place to wait for me."

A small smile touched her pretty mouth. "You forget that I found you in our barn when I brought you that pie." She reached up to touch her forehead. "Besides, you like horses—you are *gut* with them. I figured you'd come out to the barn eventually."

"And if I hadn't?"

He saw her swallow hard. "I would have found a way to talk with you alone. I would have knocked on the door and asked for you if it was the only way."

He stared at her, speechless. She looked amused as she arched an eyebrow.

"Can we talk?"

He cracked a smile. "I thought you were," he teased.

Her expression cleared as she shifted closer to him. "I have something to confess and it might make you mad."

He frowned. Dread filled him as he wondered what she had done. "What about?"

"Henry Yoder. I saw him yesterday," she said.

His chest constricted. "That's nice." He swallowed. "How is Henry?" He spoke easily, as if his heart weren't pounding in his chest and his breathing wasn't shallow.

She shrugged. "I don't think he is well. He acted strange, and I finally figured out why."

"Ja?" he replied, keeping his voice light and breezy, although he felt anything but relaxed.

"I accused him of something. I told him that I thought that it was him—and not you—who threw paint all over Bob Whittier's siding. I was right. He admitted it. I suggested that he come forward, and he refused. He said he was scared. Brad apparently threatened him with bodily harm if he told." She reached up to tug nervously on her *kapp* strings.

Isaac felt a constriction in his chest. The pounding of his heart become louder, nearly deafening in his ears. "Ellen—"

"Henry committed the crime and you took blame," she said, eyeing him closely.

He felt himself squirm under her regard. "You sound so certain."

"Henry confessed, but I always knew that you were innocent. I knew what they said about you wasn't true."

He turned away then, unable to look into Ellen's bright eyes. She seemed to regard him as a hero when he was nothing of the sort. He had lied and committed a sin. It was as simple as that.

"Isaac." Ellen's soft voice was in his ear. She had approached while he'd fought his inner demons.

"I'm not a *gut* person, Ellen," he said crossly.

"You're the person I've always known," she whispered, her breath soft against his ear. "The only one I've ever loved."

He jerked, shot her a glance, and what he saw in her blue gaze made him quiver.

"I'm not *gut* enough for you."

"Don't be ridiculous, Isaac."

He stiffened. "I'm not. I'm being reasonable."

"Like you were when I made the mistake of telling you exactly what I thought of Nancy?" She scowled. "I never told you this, Isaac, but while you were seeing her, Nancy came to me and made it clear in no uncertain terms that you were hers, and there was no room in your life for me—your little friend."

"What?"

"She was jealous, although I have no idea why. You were clearly in love with her."

"She didn't love me," he said. "Do you know what she told me when she wanted to break up? That the only reason she agreed to spend time with me was because she was curious. She said she'd been watching television shows about the Amish and she wanted to date one. She thought it would be a lark to date me because of how I was raised." He emitted a growl of displeasure. "I cared for her, but I was just a joke to her. It was her sweetness that first drew me to her, except it was all an act."

"I'm sorry, Isaac."

Ellen stood close to Isaac and felt his lingering pain and disappointment.

"You should leave now," he said. "You'd be wise to leave before I do something and hurt you without meaning to."

He didn't really want her to leave, she realized. His tone told her that he wanted her to stay. "I'm sorry, but I'm staying," she breathed. She touched his forearm, felt his arm muscle contract at her touch. "I'm not going anywhere."

He looked tortured but hopeful. "Ellen…"

She gazed at him, conveying her love for him in her smile. "I care about you, Isaac."

He suddenly stiffened, pulled away. "What about Nate?"

"What about him?"

"He likes you."

She nodded. "*Ja*, he does, but not in the way you think. We're friends. He likes someone else."

"You and Nate are just friends." His gray eyes gleamed when she nodded.

"Nate Peachy is a friend and he took me home after we—"

Isaac looked at her then.

"I don't know what we did. I only know that we need to stop avoiding the issues between us. Nate is a *gut* man, but he's not you. He'll never be you."

He blinked. "Ellen—"

"I care for you, Isaac, more than I've ever cared for anyone. I cared for you before, during and after Nancy. Why do you think I was so devastated when you didn't believe me, when you got mad because I didn't want you to be hurt?" She rubbed her temple against the onset of a headache. "You said that you missed me. Is that true?"

He nodded. "*Ja*, 'tis true."

"*Gut*, because I miss you, too."

He released a shuddering breath. "Ellen, I lied to the authorities and our community. I took the blame for something I didn't do."

"I know." She smirked. "Do you want to go back and do it for real?"

He blinked. Laughed. "I don't believe that's wise. So the truth of what I did doesn't bother you?"

"You were protecting Henry. The truth only makes me love you more." She cradled his jaw with her hand. His skin was warm and there was a stubble of whiskers on his chin. She smiled, imagining how he would look with a beard after they married.

"Ellen…" He closed his eyes as she rubbed her palm from his ear along his jaw to his chin, then up to his other ear. She felt him tremble beneath her fingers.

"Isaac, I want to spend time with you. Can you give me time?" She withdrew her hand and his eyes opened. "I want us to be honest with each other. If you don't feel for me the way I feel about you— Isaac?"

"I love you, Ellen," he said intently. "I would like to spend time with you."

Ellen experienced overwhelming joy.

"But," he went on, "I can't promise you a future."

"I'm only seventeen, Isaac. I'm too young to wed." She grinned. "Besides, I started my new job at the clinic today."

"How was it?"

"I liked it. It's only for two days a week, which gives me time to do my chores and continue my quilting. And we'll be able to spend some time together."

A light entered Isaac's eyes. Warmth filled his expression. "I'd like that."

She nodded. He reached out then and turned her to fully face him. There was understanding, tenderness and wonder in his beautiful gray eyes. "I'm happy that you like your new job, Ellen. I knew it would be a *gut* fit for you."

"But?" she asked.

"No buts," he whispered as he drew her into his arms. "I am pleased and happy."

She grinned and wrinkled her nose at him.

He laughed, a deep sound that vibrated inside his chest before it burst free and everything felt right and good to Ellen. "You'll come for dinner at my *haus* tomorrow?" she asked.

He seemed uncertain. "We'll be giving your *eldre* the wrong impression." His expression softened as he studied her. "Are you sure you want me to come?"

"*Ja*, I want you come."

He reluctantly agreed. She could tell that he was nervous about the prospect. If he came alone, it would be giving her parents the wrong idea.

"Why don't you bring Joseph and Hannah with you?"

"I don't know about Hannah…"

"Then Daniel and Joseph?"

He nodded as if it solved the problem. "*Ja*, I could bring them."

"*Gut*, then it's settled."

"I'll walk you home."

Her lips twitched. "I have the buggy."

"Then I'll drive you home."

She shook her head. "Then someone will have to drive you back."

"*Nay*, I can walk—"

"Is this the way it's going to be?" she teased. "You

always wanting to take me everywhere, worrying about every little thing? 'Tis not dark, Isaac. I'll be fine going home on my own." She gazed at him tenderly. "I will see you tomorrow." She paused. "Are you working?" She was pleased when Isaac shook his head. "Then can we meet tomorrow morning? We can go for a walk, maybe for coffee or tea somewhere."

His features softened. "Nine o'clock?" he asked. There was affection in his gray gaze.

"*Oll recht.* Where?"

"I'll come for you."

She chuckled softly as she shook her head, but she didn't argue. "I'll see you then." She wasn't surprised when he followed her closely as she headed outside.

"*Guten nacht*, Isaac," she murmured.

"*Guten nacht,*" Isaac mirrored with tenderness as his fingers caressed her cheek.

Ellen quickly pulled away and climbed into her buggy before she gave in to the urge to linger longer until it was too dark for her to drive home alone. As she left, her heart beat wildly in her chest, and she was warmed by the memory of their conversation.

I love you, Isaac. She hoped that he understood and believed it. She didn't want to scare him away. She needed him to decide for himself whether or not they were to have a future together. And she prayed and remained hopeful that God had plans that included the two of them together forever.

Chapter Eighteen

Supper at the house with the three Lapp brothers and her family was a noisy, enjoyable affair. Ellen watched with fond amusement as Isaac, Daniel and Joseph teased Will and Elam as they sat down at the table. If there was an air of awkwardness when Isaac and his siblings first arrived, it was gone within minutes of them all sitting down together at the table. Guests were always welcome at *Mam's* table. She didn't question why the Lapp boys had chosen to visit them. Before eating, they all bowed their heads and her father said a prayer to ask for the Lord's blessing of their food. Ellen peeked up to study the occupants at the table and smiled warmly as she encountered Isaac, who was doing the same thing.

Mam had prepared a number of her favorite dishes. There was roast beef and pork sausage and a bowl of chicken potpie. Ellen had helped to prepare the dried-corn casserole and mashed potatoes. She had also made the raisin bread with white frosting. If the way they were consuming their food was any indication, the young men at the table thought the meal good. Ellen smiled as she studied her brothers before her gaze settled on *Mam*. Her mother smiled and nodded. She was enjoying the company of her family and dinner guests along with her food.

As she reached for the bowl of potatoes, Ellen became conscious of her father's gaze on her. She grinned at him, pleased when he relaxed and smiled back. When her two brothers and the three Lapps took turns teasing her, she gasped and rose from her seat in outrage.

Daniel and Joseph Lapp stared at her in stunned horror, clearly believing that they'd somehow offended her.

"I'm sorry, Ellen," Joseph said.

Isaac didn't say a word as he silently studied her, amused. She blinked and tried not to let on that she was pretending. But she had a feeling that somehow he'd known.

"*Ja*, Ellen, we didn't mean anything by the things we said," Daniel said.

"We're sorry, Ellen," Elam apologized, much to Ellen's glee.

She stared at her brothers, frowned as she glanced at each and every male in the kitchen except her father and Isaac, who still hadn't said a word during the exchange.

Ellen burst out laughing. "As if you could hurt my feelings with a little teasing…" She narrowed her gaze. "But be careful. I have a long memory."

Joseph and Daniel chuckled. Elam and Will gazed at her as if she were a stranger. They'd never seen this teasing side of her before. Isaac's lips twitched as if he was holding himself back.

Ellen sat down and set to passing around the brownies she'd made for dessert. Her gaze settled on Isaac, who continued to regard her with amusement and something more. She was infused with warmth at the affection she saw in his gaze. She shot a quick glance toward her mother, who watched them both with curiosity while managing to hide her thoughts.

"Who wants custard pie?" she asked cheerfully after she'd passed around the brownie plate. She looked at the man directly across from her. "Isaac?"

Eyes gleaming, he nodded. *"Ja, danki."*

She frowned at him until his mouth stretched into a grin. She enjoyed having everyone at the table, and the realization that her father wasn't eyeing Isaac as if he were a criminal or worse made things more pleasurable.

The dinner that evening set the tone for the next several days. She and Isaac spent their every free moment together. They weren't blatant about meeting. She assumed her family would accept their friendship as they had in the past.

Isaac wasn't courting her. There was no mention of a future again, so Ellen simply welcomed the time she got to spend in his company. Ellen still sensed that Isaac was troubled by his past. He hadn't made up his mind about whether or not to stay in Happiness or leave. After a week had passed, then two, then a month, Isaac hadn't said anything about his decision, and Ellen began to worry about his leaving. She knew that she would be devastated if he chose to go. With every day, she fell deeper in love with him, and she didn't know how she would go on without him.

One night, they decided to meet in their special spot on her father's farm after they'd eaten supper in their own homes. Ellen gladdened at the sight of Isaac when she found him waiting for her on her grandfather's wooden bench. She hadn't expected him to arrive first and it pleased her immensely that he might have been anxious to see her.

"Isaac," she murmured as she drew close to him.

He stood and she gazed up into his beautiful gray eyes. "*Hallo*, Ellen," he said quietly.

Something different in his demeanor drew her attention. She experienced a cold feeling of dread.

"What's wrong?" she asked worriedly.

"We have to talk."

"About what?" She stared at him. "You made a decision."

He nodded. "Ellen—"

"You're going to leave. You've decided to leave me."

"Ellen—"

"I love you, Isaac. I want you to know that. It's not just about caring—it's about love."

"And I love you. I'll always love you."

Her eyes filled with tears. "But you're leaving." She looked away.

He grasped her shoulders, turned her to face him fully. "Now, why would I do that when I have everything I've ever wanted or needed right here?"

She blinked, saw him watching her with bright eyes. "I don't understand—"

"You. You're everything I've ever wanted."

"I am?" she whispered, filled with emotion.

"I love you, Ellen Mast." He smiled, cupped her cheek. "These last weeks have shown me that I can be happy again. You've made me happy, Ellen." He cocked his head as his lips curved into an affectionate smile. "I want to court you officially. I want to marry you someday. I understand that it can't be soon, at least, not soon enough to suit me, but with your clinic work and our ages, I know 'tis better if we wait. Besides, I have to start saving for a place for us to live."

Ellen's tears flowed unchecked down her cheeks. "Am I dreaming? Or did you just tell me that you want to court me?"

"You're awake and, *ja*, I did." He appeared confident of his decision, of their love. She started to sob loudly.

"Ellen!" he moaned. "What's wrong?"

She lifted her head and allowed him to see her longing and love for him. "Nothing's wrong, Isaac. Everything is right. I love you."

Relief had him sagging a moment with closed eyes. When he opened them again, he pulled her close and hugged her tightly. He loosened his hold but didn't let her go. "I wish—"

"Ja?" she prompted.

Isaac gazed at the woman he loved and wondered why he'd never seen it before, that Ellen Mast was perfect for him in every way. "I wish I could turn back the clock to a time before I hurt you. I wish we could start over."

"We are starting over."

He caressed her cheek. "What did I do to deserve you?" he murmured. She had saved him. He finally felt as if his life was full. He had to accept that after all this time Henry Yoder was never going to come forward with the truth. But it no longer mattered, because Ellen believed in him, and he realized that her belief and trust in him was more than enough for him.

"Are you ever going to kiss me, Isaac?" she asked softly.

He gave a jolt. He'd been longing to kiss her for

weeks now, but he hadn't wanted to do anything he shouldn't.

"We're courting now, *ja*?" she said saucily.

He stifled a grin.

"Then?" she prompted.

A tremor coursed through him as he bent to kiss her in a gentle, tender meeting of mouths. He quickly raised his head and stepped back. He saw the dreamy look on her face and felt satisfied.

"Isaac?"

"Ja?" He stepped close once again to reach out and cradle her face with his hands. "I love you."

She sighed happily. "*Gut*, because I love you."

Weeks went by and Ellen enjoyed the warm and fuzzy glow of having an attentive sweetheart. They were courting—not that anyone knew it yet. They weren't ready for marriage, so they kept their meetings private, which was what couples living in an Amish community who were in love did until they were ready to wed.

They found time to be together each day, even on the days when one or both of them worked. Sometimes it was late when they met in their special place. On certain occasions, it was Ellen who arrived first, but more times than not, it was Isaac who waited for her in the dark with some little token of his affection, like a wildflower he'd picked for her or a pretty rock he'd found at the job site. But it was the look in his eyes and the way he reached for her hand when he saw her that was the greatest gift to Ellen. She would never ask for more than Isaac's love. With him, she had everything she ever wanted or needed.

It was on a Friday morning when Isaac suggested they head to Whittier's Store for some licorice, something else they both enjoyed. Inside, Ellen waited by his side as Isaac picked out two boxes of candy. He handed her a box of Good and Plentys. Together they wandered outside to enjoy it in the warm early-summer sun.

"I should have known you were the one for me when I realized that we share the same taste in many foods," Isaac said.

"Truly grounds for a perfect match," she teased.

They sat down on the benches that Bob had added recently on the side of the store away from the parking lot. Ellen enjoyed the burst of candy coating flavor followed by the lovely taste of anise in her mouth.

"Want a soda?" Isaac asked.

She shrugged. "Maybe later. Not now."

Suddenly, Ellen suffered an awful sense of foreboding. Her stomach started to burn, the fire rising up inside her chest, down her neck and along her back even before she heard someone say his name.

"Isaac."

Ellen glanced toward the person who'd spoken, a girl with light brown hair and no makeup but with a face she'd never be able to forget.

"It's me, Isaac," she said as if confirming it. "Nancy."

Isaac appeared stunned as he rose slowly to his feet. "Nancy, what are you doing here?"

Gone were the English girl's dark hair and clothes, strange jewelry and ruby-red lips. The girl before her was a young woman so opposite in appearance from the girl Isaac had fallen for hard that he stared, dumbfounded. Nancy gazed at him like she was happy to see him…

"May I talk with you a minute?" Nancy asked softly.

Isaac glanced at Ellen before looking back. "For a minute," he said.

Nancy's back, Ellen thought. Isaac's reaction made her feel physically ill.

She watched with growing horror as the man she loved walked away to talk privately with the *Englisher*. Stricken, Ellen looked the other way, unable to watch the two of them together.

But then she had to look back. She couldn't help herself. Nancy stood with her arms out while Isaac held on to the girl's hands. They seemed to be speaking urgently, but Ellen couldn't tell what they were saying and she was afraid to guess. Was the girl asking him for forgiveness, pleading with him to give her another chance?

Isaac flashed her a glance. Ellen forced herself to smile and dip her head as if acknowledging his right to talk with the girl. He said something to Nancy, then broke away, heading in her direction. Ellen drew a fortifying breath and managed to gaze at him with unconcern as he drew near.

"I have to go with her. She needs…" He seemed reluctant to continue.

"Oll recht," she said breezily. "I can find my way home."

He shook his head. "I can drop you home on the way."

"Nay," she replied with a smile, although inside she was slowly dying. "I need to shop for a few things."

"Then I'll come back for you."

"No need. I just saw Nate's brother Jacob. I'll get a ride with him."

"I'll meet you as soon as I can."

She shrugged indifferently.

Isaac gazed at her a long moment as if hesitant to leave her. "Ellen…"

"Isaac?" Nancy urged. The girl approached. Ellen narrowed her eyes, but the *Englisher* avoided her gaze.

"I'm coming," he said, then turned to Ellen. "I'll see you later."

Ellen could only nod.

Then she watched as the man she loved with all of her heart left with his former sweetheart.

"When did this start?" Isaac asked the girl on the buggy seat beside him. He'd been shocked to see the bruises on her arms.

"Three years ago, but not as much as now."

He eyed Nancy with horror. "Brad has been hitting you, abusing you, for three years?"

Nancy blinked back tears. "Yes. It's why I asked you not to say anything that night—to take the blame for something you didn't do."

"I didn't take the blame. I just didn't defend myself. And I didn't do it for you." He paused. "I did it for Henry."

She nodded as if she understood. She looked miserable, and after hearing her story, he couldn't help but feel sorry for her. Sorry and nothing more.

I love Ellen. He realized that he'd merely been infatuated with Nancy. Just as she had been curious and interested in him because he was from an Amish household, he had been curious and interested in her, he realized, because she was English and wildly different in dress and attitude.

"Where are we going?" she asked meekly.

He still couldn't believe that this girl without makeup, black hair and dark clothes was Nancy Smith. "To someone who can help you."

"But—"

"He's a *gut* man. He will figure out how to keep you safe." He tensed his jaw. "You weren't kind to Ellen," he said.

She shook her head. "I'm sorry."

"You should be telling her."

"I owe you an apology, too."

"No need. I'm fine." And he was, because he had Ellen's love.

Nancy was silent as Isaac steered the buggy toward Abram Peachy's residence. As deacon, Abram would know what to do. Within minutes, he put on his right battery-operated turn signal and pulled into the dirt drive that lead to Abram's farmhouse.

As he pulled up and parked the buggy near the house, he saw the door to the house open and Abram, Charlotte and three of their six children exit the structure.

"Isaac!" Abram exclaimed with pleasure. "What brings you here?"

Isaac stepped out of the buggy, walked around to the other side. "I have someone who needs your help. She isn't safe at home. I was hoping you could find a safe haven for her." As he spoke, he opened the door and helped Nancy to alight.

Abram and Charlotte, he saw, were eyeing the girl with curiosity yet without censure.

"Are you in need of a safe place to stay?" Abram asked.

She nodded shyly. "Yes, sir."

"Abram." The man smiled. "Charlotte? Why don't you take…"

"Nancy," Isaac supplied, and he saw surprised understanding brighten Abram's features.

"Nancy," he said softly. "Go with my wife. We will help you. You must be hungry. We have plenty to eat. One thing we always have is *gut* food."

After Charlotte had taken the girl inside with soft words for her children to follow, Isaac found himself alone with Abram.

"Her brother hits her," he said. Then he went on to tell Abram exactly what Nancy had told him. "Check her arms, and you'll see what I mean."

Abram nodded. "We'll see that she reaches safety in a *gut* home."

Isaac bowed his head. *"Danki."* He turned to go.

"Isaac!" Abram's voice stopped him.

He turned. *"Ja?"*

"What is this girl to you?"

"Someone I once thought I knew. Now she is simply a stranger who needs help."

Abram nodded as if satisfied. Isaac started to leave and then turned back. "Abram, may I have a word with you?"

The man nodded.

"Privately?"

"Ja, you may say what you want and it will go no further unless you want it to."

Then Isaac told him what was on his mind and the good deacon listened carefully while he talked until he had nothing more to say.

Ellen was home, helping her mother with the baking. She felt frozen inside, half-numb, as she recalled

Nancy's arrival and the way Isaac had simply left her in favor of the *Englisher*.

What if he changed his mind about loving her now that Nancy was back? she wondered.

Isaac had told her he loved her. She had to trust in his love. Still, it hurt to see him with the girl.

I love you, Isaac. I want you to be happy. She stifled a sob as she rolled and then pounded fresh bread dough.

She'd hoped that he would have come by now. Why had he gone with her? What possible reason would make him urgently leave with the *Englisher*?

"Ellen," *Mam* said, "what's wrong?"

She looked at her mother, managed to smile. "I'm fine."

"*Nay*, you're not, but I won't press. You'll tell me when you're ready."

Ellen nodded, then went back to work, preparing the dough for baking.

A knock on the front door drew her and *Mam's* attention. "I'll get it," her mother said.

Ellen heard talking but couldn't distinguish the owner of the voice or the tone. Then her mother returned to the kitchen, her expression guarded. *"Mam?"*

"You've got a visitor," she said. "You'd best talk with him."

"Him?" Ellen said, feeling a nervous flutter.

"Isaac."

"I don't know—"

"Go talk with him, Ellen. The man is extremely upset. He thinks he's hurt you and he needs to see you."

Ellen raised her eyebrows. "He told you all that?"

Mam shrugged. "Just talk with him before he goes away."

Ellen quickly wiped her hands on a tea towel and hurried toward the front door.

"Isaac," she whispered as soon as she saw him.

He gazed at her with a strange sort of hunger in his eyes. "Ellen, can we talk?"

She glanced quickly over her shoulder, saw they were alone, then nodded. As she stepped outside, she was shocked when he took her hand and clasped it firmly. The warmth of his fingers against her own was nearly her undoing. He was everything to her.

Isaac led her to their special spot.

"Ellen, I'm sorry," he began.

"I understand. Nancy is back and you love her."

He looked stunned. "*Nay!* That's not true! I want you—I love only you."

"I don't understand. You left with her."

"She needed help. I took her to Abram's." His features softened. "I love you, Ellen. And I just said so to Abram."

Ellen caught her breath. "You told the deacon?" She felt the budding warmth of happiness.

He nodded. "I brought Nancy to him for protection." He assisted her onto the wooden bench, then took his seat next to her. Keeping her hand in his, he cradled it against his thigh. "Her brother, Brad—" Ellen shuddered at the name. "He's been beating her for years. I didn't realize it but it makes sense. I guess I should have known."

"Why didn't Nancy leave home before now?" she asked as joy filled the space where her pain had lodged.

"He'd never beat her this badly. You should have seen her arms—I couldn't believe it. She told her mother what he'd done, and the woman didn't believe Nancy. She chose her son over her own daughter."

Ellen gasped, her eyes filling with tears. "That's terrible."

"Ja," he said as he turned, reached out to touch her face with the back of the fingers of his other hand. "I told Abram about you. I told him I didn't know when, but that I planned to marry you, and that…" he blushed "…I thought you felt the same." He was quiet as he continued to caress her cheek while he waited for her response.

"I do want to marry you." She wondered if she could wait to have him as her husband.

"I love you, Ellen."

She felt her heart overflow with love. "Isaac Lapp, you're all I've ever wanted." She closed her eyes briefly. "I thought I'd lost you to Nancy. Again."

"Never," he replied urgently. He gazed at her with love. "I confronted Nancy about the way she treated you." He clamped his teeth together. "She didn't deny it. Said she was sorry. I told her that she should be apologizing to you."

She saw the proof of his love in his expression, naked for her to see. They were meant to be together. She'd prayed and God had answered her prayers, showing her the truth of His love.

"I love you, Isaac."

He beamed at her. "I love you, Ellen."

"Ellen!"

They heard Ellen's mother and rose to head back toward the house. Ellen felt a spring in her step that came with happiness and the wonder of loving and being loved.

As they reached the gate, Isaac stilled. "Your *eldre*."

"My parents will accept you," she said with resolve.

"I hope so. I don't want to be the cause of any more pain for you. If your *mam* and *dat* won't approve of me—"

"The only way you could hurt me is to leave me."

"I don't think I can leave you."

They walked out of the pasture and into the yard to discover her mother by the clothesline, taking down clothes.

Isaac stopped and with a grin picked up Ellen at the waist and spun her around. "I love you," he whispered. As soon as he set her down, she broke away but met his smile with a loving look of her own.

"Mam," she breathed as she felt the first raindrop. She ran to help her mother hurriedly take down her clothes.

"Ach, there you are." She smiled as Ellen unclipped clothespins as fast as her fingers could manage. To her mother—and Ellen's—shock, Isaac joined them, his masculine fingers assisting with rapid speed and skill.

"There, all finished," Isaac said. He reached down to pick up the full laundry basket. "Where would you like these?"

"In the *kiche*," *Mam* said, referring to the kitchen.

He nodded and followed them into the house. He stepped inside, set down the basket and then reached for Ellen's hand. "Josie," he said, "I'm in love with your *dochter*."

Josie studied him thoroughly and Ellen was pleased to see him gaze back at her without fear. "Well," *Mam* said, "'tis about time."

Isaac blinked. Ellen gasped. "You're not surprised?" she asked.

A soft smile settled on her mother's mouth. "You two have cared for each other for years. I was wondering if you'd ever get together—so, *ja*. 'Tis about time."

"But *Dat*—"

"What about *Dat*?" her father said as he entered the room from the front of the house. He took one look at his daughter holding hands with Isaac Lapp.

"Oh, *gut*! It finally happened."

"But I thought you disapproved of me," Isaac began.

"For that incident at Whittier's Store? We know you, Isaac. You didn't do it. You may have been protecting someone, but you yourself would never do anything to hurt a friend—and Bob Whittier is a friend."

Ellen was stunned to see Isaac's eyes glisten as if he was emotionally moved and trying to hold back tears.

"See?" Ellen said. "Like me, they never believed in your guilt. And they will come to love you as I do." When Isaac arched an eyebrow with amusement, she blushed. "Well, not as I do, but as a *soohn*."

"Will we be getting a visit from the deacon?" *Dat* asked.

"You can count on it," Isaac said, much to Ellen's delight.

Epilogue

A year later, on a sunny day during the month of November, Isaac and Ellen stood before their families and the entire church congregation to pledge their love for each other as they wed. Ellen's cousin Mary Ruth had come for their special day. Ellen was glad to see her and took her cousin's ribbing about Isaac good-naturedly.

No one witnessing the event could doubt the bride and groom's love and their commitment to each other.

Although Isaac had remained silent on the subject of Whittier's Store, the truth finally had come out when Henry Yoder confessed his role in the crime to the church elders and then later to Bob Whittier. His confession didn't come immediately; it happened well after Josie and William Mast had given their approval and blessing for Isaac and Ellen's marriage.

During the past year, Ellen had continued her work at the Westmore Clinic. She enjoyed doing her part to help special children and she would continue there into the future, at least for a little while. Now she wanted nothing more than a life with Isaac and to give her husband children—lots of them.

All the members of the Lapp family stood by, watching with love and joy as Isaac wed his beautiful Ellen. Like the Masts, they had always believed in Isaac's innocence, but they had been waiting for him to come to them with the truth. They didn't approve of his taking the blame for Henry, but they understood why Isaac had kept silent about his friend.

As he stood next to his lovely bride, Isaac felt a peace and happiness he'd never expected to feel again.

"Ellen," Isaac whispered as he leaned close before they headed outside to the vehicle that would take them to the William Mast farmhouse, where a wedding feast would be provided for all.

"Ja?" she breathed, looking deeply into his eyes. She would never grow tired of gazing into those gray orbs, of standing at Isaac's side, of feeling the warmth of his touch.

"I love you, Ellen Lapp," he murmured as he dipped his head to brush his lips against her forehead.

Thrilled to hear her new surname, Ellen gazed lovingly at her groom, then leaned close to whisper, "Isaac, my dear husband, I love you even more."

* * * * *

Dear Reader,

Welcome to Happiness, Pennsylvania, home to the Samuel Lapps and many other wonderful Amish families. Samuel Lapp and his wife, Katie, have seven sons and a daughter. Their family, as well as their neighbors and friends, drew me from the first moment I started to see them come alive on paper.

Saving Isaac is the fifth novel in my Lancaster County Weddings series. It features Isaac Lapp and his relationship with Ellen Mast. Ellen and Isaac were once close friends until Isaac met and fell for Nancy Smith, an English girl. From the moment he became involved with the *Englisher*, he thought only of that girl. Because of his blind infatuation with Nancy, Isaac unintentionally hurt Ellen when he abandoned their friendship. Two years have passed and Isaac is no longer with Nancy. Because of trouble he found with the girl's brother and friends, Isaac struggles with a lack of self-worth and with the decision of whether to join the Amish church and stay in his Amish community or leave to live life elsewhere. He realizes that he hurt Ellen badly by abandoning their friendship. Determined to make amends, Isaac is soon faced with another dilemma as he finds himself with unexpected feelings for Ellen, a young woman destined to join the Amish church and remain in Happiness. Isaac doesn't believe that he can do the same.

I wish you the best that life has to offer. May the Lord bless and keep you safely within His loving arms. Love and light,
Rebecca Kertz

"What can I do for you, Officer?" Josie Markham's tone
said she didn't really want to do anything for him. Ever.

He raised his eyebrows.

"White hat. Boots. White starched shirt. And that
belt's the type they only issue to Texas Rangers." She
gestured toward his holster. "I hope you weren't trying
to be undercover."

"Good eye." He extended his hand. She narrowed
her gaze but shook it. "Heath Grayson. I'm a friend of
Flint's."

In the space of a heartbeat, her hesitant expression
vanished and was replaced by wide-eyed concern. "Did
something else happen at the boys ranch?" She shifted
from around the wheelbarrow. "What are we waiting for?
If something's wrong, let's go."

Once she moved away from the wheelbarrow, he
saw her stomach. Pregnant. Very pregnant. Flint had
mentioned Josie was widowed, but he'd left out the little
detail that she was with child. So a recent widow.

Had she been in the barn alone…doing chores?

"Let me help you with your chores," Heath said.

Josie's jaw dropped. "What about the boys ranch?"

"The ranch is fine."

"Why didn't you say so? You about gave me a heart attack." She laid her hand on her chest and took a few deep breaths. Then her eyes skirted back up to capture his. "If the ranch is fine, why exactly are you here then?"

She fanned her face and dragged in huge amounts of oxygen through her mouth as if she was having a hard time getting it into her lungs.

Now he'd done it. Gone and gotten a pregnant woman all worked up. Did he need to find her a chair? A drink of water? Rush her to the hospital? What a terrible feeling, being out of control. It was disconcerting.

"Are you all right, ma'am? What do you need?"

"I'm fine. Just fine." She laughed. "You should see your face, though." She pointed up at him and covered her mouth, hiding her wide grin. Her warm brown eyes shone with mischief. "Now you look like you're the one having a heart attack. Relax there, Officer. It was only a figure of speech." Her laugh was a high sound, full of joy. Josie laughed with her whole self, without holding anything back.

Heath wanted to hear it again.

Don't miss
THE RANGER'S TEXAS PROPOSAL
by Jessica Keller, available November 2016 wherever
Love Inspired® books and ebooks are sold.

www.LoveInspired.com